T0209163

SAVED FOR BEN:

THE COLLEGE YEARS

JACQUELYN B. SMITH

WESTBOW
PRESS®
A DIVISION OF THOMAS NELSON
& ZONDERVAN

WestBow Press books may be ordered through booksellers or by contacting:

WestBow Press
A Division of Thomas Nelson & Zondervan
1663 Liberty Drive
Bloomington, IN 47403
www.westbowpress.com
844-714-3454

ISBN: 978-1-6642-6890-6 (sc)
ISBN: 978-1-6642-6892-0 (hc)
ISBN: 978-1-6642-6891-3 (e)

Library of Congress Control Number: 2022911125

Print information available on the last page.

WestBow Press rev. date: 07/27/2022

This *Saved for Ben* series is dedicated to my loving and nurturing grandmother, Ora Lee Woods; a second to none mother, Lillie Mae Wood; and my village. My grandmother and mother used every opportunity available to broaden my horizons and instill life changing godly principles in me. God has connected wonderful people to my journey of spiritual growth. My village consists of those who have prayed, encouraged, and helped me during my journey of academic years, military service, and personal growth whether in Georgia, Virginia, Texas, or Florida. I am forever grateful for their love, support, and endearing friendship. Last but now least, to my son, Jeremy, a precious gift of God, who has inspired me to continue making a difference through writing for those who are willing to trust God.

CONTENTS

1

BEN ARRIVES AT THE UNIVERSITY

B en finally stopped crying by the time he was five miles outside of the city limits of Fairville. The drive to Middle Georgia State University in Macon was very pleasurable, his 1970 Ford F-150 was equipped with air condition. Ben was glad his mother packed him lunch, he was getting hungry. He was excited about everything. He wondered if his roommate would be from Georgia or up north. It was possible that his roommate could be an international student.

As he was about to turn into the entrance of the university, he saw a pay phone. He decided to go ahead and call Mr. Cason, so his family would not be worried about him.

He had only been gone a few hours, but he relished in hearing Mr. Cason's voice. As he drove up to Martin Hall's parking lot, it was filled with students and their families. He parked the truck and went inside to check in. The housing representative gave him his key and told him that his roommate had not checked in yet.

Ben took his time and transported all of his possessions to his room. He tried not to pack too much. He had clothing, toiletries, bedding, school supplies, and some family pictures. He also brought a desk lamp, so he would not have to use the overhead light all of the time. He was assigned to room 343. During the campus tour Tammy, the tour guide, said that most freshmen were assigned to the third floor. As he was going back and forth to the truck, several students introduced themselves. His resident assistant was Dale Henderson. Dale was tall with blond hair and a junior engineering major from Raleigh, North Carolina.

Finally, after about two hours, Ben had unpacked all of his belongings and set up his side of the room. He tried to wait for his roommate, he wanted to give him first option of the side of the room. He could not wait any longer; so, he took the right side. Then he heard a faint knock at the door. As he was turning around, a student was entering the room.

Ben smiled and said, "Hi, my name is Ben Davis."

The student said, "I am Charles Hemingway, III from Charleston, South Carolina. Are you in the right room?"

Shocked Ben said, "Yes, I am. I'm assigned to room 343 Martin Hall."

Charles said vehemently, "Well, then I cannot stay here. I will not share my room with a colored boy!"

Ben was speechless. He couldn't move. He just looked at Charles.

Charles continued, "I have to go find the resident assistant."

Charles stood in the hallway, yelling at the top of his voice, "Has anyone seen the resident assistant? Resident assistant! Resident assistant!"

In a few moments, Dale appeared at the door.

Dale said, "I'm Dale Henderson, I am your resident assistant. Is there a problem?"

Charles berated, "Yes, there is a problem. I will not share my room with a colored person!"

Dale asked politely, "What is your name?"

Charles said proudly, "I am Charles Hemingway, III from the Charleston Hemingways."

Dale asked, "May I call you Charles?"

Smiling Charles said, "Of course!"

Dale continued, "Charles, according to my manifest you have been assigned to room 343 with Benjamin Davis. If you have a problem with your assignment, you need to check with the dorm coordinator downstairs, Mr. Clark. However, I can tell you now, the dorm is full. There is no other room available."

Pushing Dale aside and visibly displeased Charles said, "Excuse me, I will go talk to this Mr. Clark. My father is in the car, we will see about this."

Charles stormed down the hall dragging his heavy luggage.

Dale looked at Ben and said, "Ben, consider yourself lucky that he doesn't want to be your roommate."

Ben smiled and said, "I am still in shock. I hoped me and my roommate would be good friends."

Dale said seriously, "Charles Hemingway the third does not seem like he will be anyone's good friend. He's extremely censorious and hubris, but he is definitely not a hypocrite."

Ben smiled. Someone else was calling for the resident assistant.

Dale said laughingly, "I really do love my job," as he walked down the hall to solve another problem.

Ben closed the door and sat on the bed.

He prayed, "God, I don't know what just happened. I trust that what you have for me is for me."

After a little while, there was another knock at the door. Ben opened the door.

The man said, "I am Mr. Clark, the dorm director. Your assigned roommate, Charles Hemingway III, does not want to share a room with you. I informed him and his father that this room was his only choice. All of the dorms are full. His father was very disparaging and livid. He has decided to take Charles back to Charleston, South Carolina. Charles was also accepted into Clemson University. So, they plan to stop by Clemson on their way home."

Ben stood there, he was still speechless.

Mr. Clark said, "Ben, we do not condone that type of behavior here at Middle Georgia State University. It is 1975 and we try to embrace equality."

Ben said, "I appreciate that."

Mr. Clark said, "Since your roommate plans to withdraw from the university. You will have this room to yourself for the school year."

Ben inquired, "Will that cost more? I am on a scholarship."

Mr. Clark smiled and said, "No, there will be no additional charge to you. Enjoy your private room. Most of the students are going to be envious. You can move the furniture around as you like, since you do not have a roommate."

Ben smiled and asked, "Is the cafeteria open today?"

Mr. Clark said, "No! However, it will be open all day tomorrow."

Ben said, "Thank you for the information."

Mr. Clark said, "Oh, I have class schedules downstairs for all freshmen students. Stop by when you can to pick up yours. You also need to get a university identification card before you go to the cafeteria. You can get one in Building 22 until six o'clock today."

Ben said, "Yes sir, I will."

Mr. Clark left the room. It was now four o'clock. Ben

grabbed his keys and left the room. As he was walking out of the door, two guys were standing in the hallway.

The white guy said, "Hi, my name is Joshua Parks, business major."

The other guy was black, he said, "My name is Caleb Champion. I am an engineering major."

Ben smiled and said, "I'm Ben Davis; I'm also a business major."

Joshua asked, "Ben, where are you headed?"

Ben said, "I need to go get a university identification card."

Caleb said, "We are headed there too. You want to walk with us?"

Ben laughed and said, "Considering I don't know which way to go, I would like that."

Everyone laughed and walked down the hall.

After picking up their class schedules, they discovered they have some classes together. They all have College Algebra together and Ben and Caleb have English together. Caleb and Joshua have History together. They each have fifteen credit hours, five different classes.

They laughed as they walked the campus. They walked around to locate the different buildings where the classes will be held. Ben was scheduled for three morning classes on Monday, Wednesday, and Friday. On Tuesday and Thursday, he was scheduled for two classes. All of his classes would be over every day by eleven o'clock in the morning.

Since the cafeteria was not open, several students were walking to a place called the Chicken Shack off campus at the back entrance of the university. Ben, Joshua, and Caleb decided to walk there too. After eating, everyone walked back to the dorm, and sat around the common area, and talked until eleven o'clock that night. It was a great first day.

Sunday was another great day in the dorm. There was a dorm meeting. Mr. Clark distributed a checklist to all of the freshmen. This list contained places that each student had to check in. They had to check in at places such as Identification Card office, Finance Office, parking office, etc. Ben met so many people. He felt good and accepted. He missed his family but he really enjoyed his private room. Having Joshua and Caleb right next door was like having two roommates.

Joshua was from Atlanta and Caleb was from Valdosta. Neither of them had heard of Fairville, the small town that Ben was from. Ben was excited about the first day of classes. This was why he was here! His plan was to complete his degree in four years, that meant taking at least five courses each semester and not failing anything.

After class on Monday, Ben walked the beautiful campus. It was full of activity. He noticed a sign at the Tutoring Center. They needed volunteers.

He walked in and said, "My name is Ben Davis. I am interested in volunteering."

The student helper said, "You need to talk to Miss Tiffany. Please have a seat."

Ben sat and waited patiently.

Miss Tiffany said, "Hello, my name is Tiffany Jolly. How are you?"

Ben said, "I am fine. I saw your sign about needing volunteers."

Miss Tiffany asked, "What year are you?"

Ben said, "I am a freshman, business major."

Miss Tiffany said, "Well, Ben usually we don't let freshmen tutor other students. However, because we are in such a crunch right now, I am willing to consider it. Are you willing to take a placement test to see what you would be able to tutor other students in?"

Ben replied, "Yes ma'am!"

Miss Tiffany said, "In order to be a tutor you have to pass the test with a score of eighty-nine percent. The test is given in two parts. I can give you the first part now and you can take the second part tomorrow afternoon."

Ben said, "That would be fine."

Miss Tiffany took Ben to a private room and administered part one of the test. When Ben was finished, he gave Miss Tiffany the answer sheet.

Miss Tiffany said, "Ben, you did not use all of your time. You don't want to look over the questions some more."

Ben said, "No ma'am. Overall, I am happy with my answers."

Miss Tiffany asked, "Can you stop by around the same time tomorrow so you can take part two of the test."

Ben replied, "Yes ma'am. I will see you tomorrow."

On the next day, Ben took the second part of the test.

Miss Tiffany said, "Ben, if you like I can grade your test now. Do you have time?"

Ben said politely, "Yes ma'am, I can wait."

After about twenty minutes Miss Tiffany said surprisingly, "Ben, you scored ninety-seven percent on the math and ninety-six percent on the English. What math and English classes are you taking now?"

Ben said, "I have College Algebra and College English."

Miss Tiffany said, "Ben, according to your tests, you could CLEP those courses if you like."

Confused Ben asked, "What does CLEP mean?"

Miss Tiffany said, "CLEP means College Level Examination Program. It's a test that if you make a score of at least fifty percent you can skip those classes and still receive credit for the courses."

Ben said hesitantly, "Oh, I don't know. When would I have to take the CLEP test?"

Miss Tiffany said, "You already took them. Those two tests I gave you are the CLEP tests for College Algebra and College English."

Ben asked, "Oh! What classes would I take if I did not take College Algebra and English?"

Miss Tiffany said, "That would depend on your major. You need to stop by the Business building and ask to see Dean Smith. He will help you make a decision."

Ben said, "Miss Tiffany, this is so unexpected. I have Algebra and English with two of my friends and I was excited about that."

Miss Tiffany said, "Ben, you can stay in your current classes, but you will not find them challenging. You already know the material. Can you call home to talk to a parent about this decision?"

Ben said, "Yes ma'am. I'll call home."

Miss Tiffany said enthusiastically, "Ben, we would love for you to come back to the Tutoring Center to help us out. You can volunteer whenever you like."

Ben said, "I would love to help you out; let me talk to Dean Smith first."

Miss Tiffany said, "No problem. See you soon."

As soon as Ben left the center, Miss Tiffany called Dean Smith on the phone to explain the situation. When Ben arrived at the College of Business Building, Dean Smith was waiting in the hallway.

Smiling Dean Smith asked, "Are you Benjamin Davis, Freshman?"

Ben smiled and said, "Yes sir. How do you know my name?"

Dean Smith laughed and said, "I just got off the phone

with Tiffany Jolly. She told me about your scores on the CLEP. Please step into my office."

Ben smiled and followed him into an office.

Impressed Ben said, "Sir, this is a very nice office."

Dean Smith said proudly, "Thank you Ben. I like it too."

Ben said sadly, "Sir, I really don't know what to do."

Dean Smith said reassuringly, "I am here to help you make the best decision for you. Tiffany is right, you have scored high enough on the CLEP exams to skip those two courses. Really it would be three courses. Normally, students take two semesters of College English. You will earn credit hours for those classes. This is a list of the courses you need to take over the next few years. So, looking at this list, we can see what classes are available now that you can take."

Ben said, "Dean Smith, I tried to explain to Miss Tiffany that I just met some guys that I have become friends with. We are all in Algebra and English together. I was really excited about that."

Dean Smith said, "Ben, I know you want to make friends. However, I am sure those guys will still be your friends, even though you are not in the same classes."

Ben contemplated then said sadly, "That is true. Dean Smith, may I use your phone to call home?"

Dean Smith said, "Of course you can, this is a big decision."

Dean Smith placed the desk phone closer to Ben and said, "Dial nine first to get an outside line, then dial one and the phone number with area code."

Ben dialed the number to the golf shop.

Mr. Cason answered, "Cason Golf Shop, may I help you?"

Ben said, "Hello Mr. Cason!"

Mr. Cason said happily, "Ben, I'm so glad you called. Are you OK?"

Ben said, "Yes sir, I'm well. I need some advice."

Mr. Cason asked seriously, "What's going on?"

Ben filled Mr. Cason in on what happened and how he had to decide about skipping the three courses or staying in the class with Joshua and Caleb.

Mr. Cason said lovingly, "Ben, I can see how you can be torn. The decision is somewhat easy, don't you think?"

Ben said, "Yes sir. Dean Smith said that he is sure the guys will still be my friends even if I'm not in class with them."

Mr. Cason said, "I agree!"

Ben said, "I just don't want them to ostracize me."

Mr. Cason said, "I don't think they will. They sound like fine boys, so I'm sure they will be happy for you."

Ben said, "Yes sir. Dean Smith said that he would help me decide what courses I should take instead of Algebra and English."

Mr. Cason said, "It sounds like Dean Smith is being very helpful."

Ben said, "Yes sir!"

Mr. Cason asked, "Is he there? Can I speak with him?"

Ben said, "Yes sir, hold on!"

Ben went to the hallway and told Dean Smith that Mr. Cason wanted to talk to him.

Dean Smith took the receiver and said, "Hello, Mr. Cason."

Mr. Cason said, "I just wanted to thank you for the help you are providing Ben. He's a special young man."

Dean Smith smiled and said, "He is very impressive."

Mr. Cason said, "I know you have hundreds of students, but would you continue to check on him from time to time. He is a good student and a very hard worker."

Dean Smith said, "It will be an honor."

Mr. Cason said, "Please tell Ben that I am very proud of him and will talk to him soon."

Dean Smith said, "Of course, have a good afternoon."

Mr. Cason said, "Goodbye!"

Dean Smith hung up the phone, smiled, and said, "Ben, that man cares a lot about you. He wanted me to tell you that he is very proud of you and that he would talk to you soon."

Ben said, "I love him very much."

Dean Smith said, "Well, while you were on the phone, I found two classes with vacancies. The classes meet during the same time slots."

Ben said, "Thank you sir, I will CLEP Algebra and English."

Dean Smith said, "You have made a wise decision. That means you already have nine credit hours. Congratulations! You have only been in college for two days."

Ben laughed.

Dean Smith said, "Macro Economics and Calculus with Business Applications are the two courses that meet during the same time periods this semester, so changing out those classes will be no problem."

Ben said, "That will be fine. I had planned to go pick up my text books today; good I had not picked them up yet."

Dean Smith smiled and said, "I will let the new and old instructors know what happened. Before you leave today, we will also change your schedule and print out a new class schedule for you."

Ben said, "Thank you sir."

Dean Smith asked, "Are you still going to volunteer at the Tutoring Center?"

Ben said, "I will since my schedule did not change."

Dean Smith said, "That is great. Have you made an appointment with your Financial Advisor?"

Ben said, "No sir, it is on my list."

Dean Smith said, "Let me call and see if he can see you now?"

Ben said, "Thank you!"

Dean Smith hung up the phone and said, "Your Financial Advisor is Kyle Culver. His office is in the Registrar, Building 100, over near the cafeteria. He is a very nice man, you will like him. He would like for you to come right over."

Ben said, "Everyone has been very nice to me so far."

Dean Smith, "I'm glad to hear that. See you later!"

Ben said, "Yes sir. Thank you for everything."

Ben left the Business building and was walking toward the Registrar. His two friends saw him and ran to meet him.

Caleb said excitedly, "Ben, we're headed to the book store to purchase our textbooks. Did you get your text books yet?"

Ben said, "No, I have not picked them up. I need to go see my Financial Advisor before I go."

Joshua asked, "Are you on scholarship?"

Ben replied, "Yes I am."

Caleb said, "Me too!"

Ben smiled and said, "I also just found out that I can CLEP College Algebra and English?"

Joshua exclaimed, "Wow, that's great!"

Caleb said, "I thought you were interested in tutoring?"

Ben said, "I am, that's how I found out that I can CLEP the courses."

Joshua asked, "So, does that mean when we need help, you will help us?

Ben smiled and replied, "Anytime!"

Caleb said, "That's great. We will see you back in the dorm later. Maybe we can eat dinner together around five o'clock."

Ben said happily, "That would be great."

As Ben continued to walk toward the Registrar, he realized that he had been worried for nothing. He thanked God for Joshua and Caleb. He knew that they would be great friends. As he entered Building 100, he did not know which way to go. Ben greeted the receptionist, "I'm looking for Mr. Kyle Culver's office."

The receptionist said, "Please have a seat. I will let him know that you are here. What is your name?"

Ben replied, "Benjamin Davis."

Ben took a seat and before he could get comfortable, Mr. Culver walked into the lobby and introduced himself. Ben followed him into his office.

Mr. Culver said, "Ben, please have a seat. I understand that you have had some excitement today."

Ben said, "Yes, sir. I am still in shock."

Mr. Culver said, "Well, I am here to add to your excitement."

Ben sat up straight and leaned forward.

Mr. Culver said, "Ben, as a scholarship recipient, each semester I need you to come by and see me. My job is to make sure you are not having any problems with your grades, housing, or anything else."

Ben replied, "Yes, sir."

Mr. Culver asked, "Do you remember completing the forms for federal grants?"

Ben said, "Yes sir! I thought since I received the scholarship, it was not an issue."

Mr. Culver said, "Even though you received the scholarship, you are still entitled to receive the federal grant money. I have for you now two checks. One is from BEOG and the other is from SEOG."

Ben said, "Sir, I don't know what that is."

Mr. Culver explained, "BEOG is the Basic Educational

Opportunity Grant and SEOG is the Supplemental Educational Opportunity Grant. Due to your family's income status, you have been awarded both grants. Since your scholarship pays for everything, those grants will be paid directly to you. However, during the school year, you cannot work on campus."

Ben said, "Sir, I remember one of my mentors telling me about the grants. If I did not get the scholarship, they could be used to pay for my tuition."

Mr. Culver said, "That is true. Since you have the scholarship, these checks are paid directly to you. Use this money for whatever you need while you are in college. Do you have a bank account?"

Ben said, "Yes sir. I have a savings account at First National Bank of Georgia."

Mr. Culver said, "Then you need to take these two checks there as soon as you can. I don't want you to lose them."

Mr. Culver passed two sealed envelopes to Ben.

Taking the envelopes, Ben stood up and said, "Sir, I am still a little confused. These checks are for me?"

Mr. Culver said, "Yes, use this money wisely for whatever you need this semester."

Ben said, "Thank you sir."

Mr. Culver said, "If you have any issues, just come to see me. If not, I will see you again during the first week of school next semester. Then you can pick up your checks for that semester."

Shocked Ben asked, "Are you saying I will receive this each semester?"

Mr. Culver said, "Yes. These checks are based on your family income level. I understand that you are being raised by a single mother and you have two younger siblings."

Ben said, "Yes sir."

Mr. Culver stood up and said, "OK, take care of yourself." Ben shook his hand and left the office in a daze. When Ben was outside of the building, he sat down on one of the benches. He opened the first envelope, inside was a check payable to Benjamin Davis for $1,500. Ben gasped. He opened the second envelope and there was a check payable to Benjamin Davis for $1,200. Ben was speechless. As he looked around he saw students coming and going. He realized that God's blessing had exceeded all that he could imagine. He was enrolled at the university. He had a scholarship that would take care everything. He also had money for any incidentals he may need. He walked to the dorm parking lot, got in his truck, and drove to the bank.

2

BALANCING ASSIGNMENTS AND FUN IS NOT EASY

B en was scheduled for his two new classes on Wednesday. In Calculus and Economics, he was already a day behind. He spent most of the night reading the first chapter of each textbook. As he walked into the Calculus classroom, Professor Drucilla James met him with a smile.

She said, "Ben, I am glad that you have chosen our class."

Ben smiled.

She said, "There are some vacant seats in the front if you like."

Ben sat down in the front row. At the end of the class, he realized that Calculus was not going to be a cake walk. As he walked out the door, he heard someone call his name. When he turned around, he saw Tammy, the tour guide.

Tammy asked, "Ben, do you remember me?"

Ben smiled and said, "Of course I do."

Tammy said, "I have been dragging my feet about taking this class. I was supposed to take it last year, but I was not ready."

Ben said, "I can see that it will be challenging."

Tammy said, "Yes, I heard that Professor James seems nice. However, she really dumps a lot of assignments and tests on the students. She is the only teacher that teaches this class for Business students, so there is no avoiding her."

Ben asked, "Wow, would you like to be study partners?"

Tammy said, "Yes, I would. Thanks! What other classes do you have?"

Ben said, "I have Macro Economics, Environmental Science, Art Appreciation, and a speech class."

Tammy said, "Well, I got an A in Macro Economics so if you need some help, just ask. The speech class does help with all of the public speaking we have to do as business majors. The art class is interesting but easy. I did not take Environmental Science, I took Biology."

Ben said happily, "Thanks Tammy! I have to go to my next class, see you later!"

By the end of the week, Ben was tired. He was volunteering at the Tutoring Center on Tuesday, Wednesday, and Thursday from 1:00 pm to 4:00 pm. Even though he liked being finished with his classes by 11:00 am, he did not like starting them at eight o'clock in the morning. Ben was learning quickly to say goodnight to his friends and go to bed. The weekend was finally here. Caleb, Ben, and Joshua were talking in the hallway.

Joshua said, "I heard about a party at one of the fraternities tonight. Do you all want to go?"

Caleb exclaimed, "Yeah I do. I heard that frat parties draw a lot of girls!"

Ben said hesitantly, "I don't think so."

Joshua whined, "Come on Ben, you may have a good time."

Ben asked unenthusiastically, "What time is the party?"

Joshua replied, "Ten o'clock!"

Ben said, "OK, I will go! Is it on campus?"

Joshua said, "No, but it's right behind the Chicken Shack, so we can walk."

Caleb said, "We will stop by your room to pick you up."

Ben knew that he needed to complete some assignments before he went to the party. Professor James, the Calculus professor, had already started dumping. Ben was scheduled to study with Tammy at 6:00 pm.

Tammy met Ben at the library to study. Ben had finished most of his Calculus assignments, but he was confused about a few questions. Tammy arrived at the library on time. Ben told her about the party he and his friends planned to attend.

Tammy advised, "Ben, be very careful at those parties. Don't eat or drink anything. Some of those fraternities spike the punch and put drugs in the food."

Shocked Ben said, "Really, I didn't know."

Tammy said, "I went to a few my freshman year, but I learned the hard way not to drink their punch."

Ben said, "OK, thanks for the heads up."

Ben helped Tammy with some of the problems, she did not know how to do. Together they were able to figure out the problems Ben was confused about.

At 10:00 pm exactly, Caleb and Joshua knocked on the door. Ben was ready. They laughed and talked all the way to the party. Ben shared the information that Tammy had told him.

Joshua said, "That's good to know, but I think I want to try some of the punch."

Caleb said, "Not me, I'm only here for the ladies!"

The party was OK. Ben did not like being around a lot of people that were drinking; some were drunk. Finally, around 12:30 am, Ben convinced his friends that it was time to go. The curfew was extended for students in the dorm on Friday and Saturday night until 1:00 am.

Caleb and Ben had to hold on to Joshua. He drank a lot of the spiked punch; he was very tipsy. Caleb bragged about how many names and dorm room numbers he got from some of the ladies.

By the time they walked back to the dorm, Joshua was throwing up everywhere. It was hard work trying to stay clear of his projectiles. Caleb and Ben got Joshua in bed, he complained about a headache and hunger.

Ben was determined to take a shower before he went to bed. On Saturday, Ben slept late. After lunch, he wanted to drive around town to see some of the sights. He invited Caleb and Joshua, but they did not want to go.

Ben set out to see Macon, Georgia. He drove around trying not to get lost. He was impressed by all of the shops. There were grocery stores and drug stores on every other block. He had never seen so many places to shop. He drove past the historical parks. Mary, his sister, had visited the Museum of Arts and Sciences but there were at least three other museums in the city. There was a new shopping mall. It had just opened in April 1975. It had over one hundred stores in one location. It was called Macon Mall. Ben ate lunch at a fast food place called McDonalds. It was different but delicious.

Ben was amazed at all of the people that lived in Macon. He wished his family could see all of the sights. He missed them. He planned to go home the upcoming Labor Day weekend. He would not have to return to college until Monday evening. He decided to purchase a few things from the university bookstore to take home as gifts. When he finally made it back to his dorm room, it was 7:00 pm. It had been a long day, but he had fun. He seemed to always have homework. As soon as he thought he was caught up, a professor would dump more on him. Just when he got comfortable in his room, Caleb and Joshua were knocking at the door.

Ben opened the door smiled and said, "Hi guys!"

Joshua and Caleb rushed into the room. Joshua said, "There's another party tonight at the sorority house. Would you like to go?"

Ben said, "No thank you. I did not like the party last night."

Caleb said, "I didn't either, but what else is there to do but go to parties."

Ben said, "When I was out today, I saw a movie theater. The new movie, Jaws, is out."

Joshua said, "We can go to a movie anytime. I want to go to the party!"

Caleb suggested, "Why don't we do both. I'm sure a movie starts around 9:00 pm, we can catch that movie, then go to the party. The party does not start until 10:30 tonight."

Ben said, "I want to go to the movie, but I'm not excited about the party. I was not comfortable being around so many people that drank. I was not brought up like that."

Joshua said, "Ben, you just don't know how to have fun."

Caleb asked, "Ben, will you drive us to the movies?"

Ben said, "Yeah, no problem. Let's leave around 8:30 pm."

Joshua negotiated, "I will go, but that means you all will go to the party with me."

Ben said, "I can't promise that."

The movie was awesome. Caleb and Ben swore they were never going swimming in the ocean. Joshua was just glad the movie was over; he was ready to go to the party. Ben drove to the party. There were girls everywhere. They mingled for a little while. Next thing you know, Joshua was drinking again.

Ben told Caleb, "I don't like it when Joshua drinks. This will be the last party I attend with him."

Caleb agreed, "I don't like it either. However, I don't want to abandon him, he's my friend. We're roommates."

Ben said, "I know. I like him too, when he's not drinking!"

Finally, the party was closing down around 12:30 am, they all piled into Ben's truck. Ben was afraid Joshua was going to throw up again.

He kept telling Joshua, "Man, don't throw up in my truck!"

When he parked the truck, Joshua was the first to get out. He threw up all over the parking lot.

Ben said seriously, "Joshua, I will not go to another party with you. I don't like it when you drink. You don't know when to stop. You keep drinking and drinking until you get sick. I really want to be your friend, but I don't like this."

Caleb agreed, "Ben is right Joshua. If you can't control yourself, I won't be attending any more parties with you either."

Joshua whined, "You all are just party poopers that don't know how to have fun."

Ben said sternly, "I want to have fun, but watching you drink excessively is not fun. I'm going to my room."

Joshua was staggering; Caleb was trying to help him. Ben did not look back. When he got to his room, he got on his knees and prayed for Joshua. He realized that he wanted friends, but he did not want friends that did not have the same morals or values as he did. Mr. Cason told him that would be an issue.

When Joshua finally got up on Sunday, he knocked on Ben's door.

Ben opened the door, smiled, and said, "Hi Joshua! Are you feeling better?"

Joshua said, "Caleb and I talked all night. I realized that I was wrong to make you guys feel bad about not drinking. I'm sorry. I'm not ready to give up drinking; so, I will find some other guys to go to parties with me. I still want you to be my friend."

Ben said, "No problem. I just didn't like being bullied to do something that I did not want to do."

Joshua said, "You're right. Friends?"

Ben smiled and said, "Yeah, friends!"

Ben, Joshua, and Caleb walked to the cafeteria for lunch. Afterwards, they walked to areas of the campus that they had not seen. The campus had a lake. They rode in the paddle boats laughing while looking for sharks. They had a great time.

3

FAVOR AND BLESSINGS

It was the second week of college. Ben liked his schedule. Even though he had to wake up early, he liked having all of his classes over by 11:00 am. He volunteered at the Tutoring Center on Tuesday, Wednesday, and Thursday from one o'clock to four o'clock. He always had an appointment. Miss Tiffany told him, that when he did not have a tutoring appointment, he could do his own homework. It had only been a couple of days that he had volunteered, but everyone wanted him as a tutor. Tutoring sessions were twenty-five minutes. As soon as one student left, he had another student waiting. The word had gotten out about how patient and knowledgeable he was.

One day Miss Tiffany said, "Ben, more students have signed up for tutoring since last week and they all want you to tutor them. You are making a name for yourself."

Ben smiled and said, "I don't know if that is good or bad."

Miss Tiffany said, "I will try to give you a break five to ten minutes after each session, so you can catch your breath."

Ben smiled and said, "That would be great. How many tutors do you have?

Miss Tiffany said, "Not enough. I need at least five more."

Ben said laughingly, "Well, I will pray for more. My mom says we have not because we ask not."

Ben left the room for his next session. The door opened and Dean Smith walked in.

He said, "Miss Tiffany, I heard that Ben Davis is doing a great job over here."

Surprised Tiffany asked, "How did you hear that?"

Dean Smith said, "A couple of the business students were talking about him. I figured I needed to come and check it out."

Tiffany smiled and said, "Well sir, he is doing a great job. I am booked for all of September and October with appointments for him."

Dean Smith inquired, "Why does everyone want him to tutor them?"

Tiffany said, "Sir, he is very knowledgeable, competent, and patient. He is not a braggart. He listens to what problems the students are having and explains to them what they are doing wrong."

Dean Smith said, "Maybe you should get him to do a training session for all of your tutors, so they can emulate him and be just as effective."

Tiffany agreed, "That's a great idea. I will plan some team training."

Dean Smith said laughingly, "If he continues at this pace, I may have to bring him over to the Business department and have him train my tutors."

Finally, it was Friday, eleven o'clock. Class was out, the truck was packed, and Ben was headed home to Fairville. He was excited to see his family. Mom would be at work when he got home and his siblings, David and Mary, would be in school. So, he decided to go straight to the golf shop.

He parked the truck in front of the store. When he walked through the door, Mr. Cason was checking out a customer with another one waiting. Ben did not want to interrupt, but Mr. Cason stopped what he was doing and rushed to hug him.

Mr. Cason said proudly, "Everyone, this is Ben!"

Each of the customers said hello and shook his hand.

One customer said, "It's nice to meet you Ben; Charlie talks about you all the time."

The other customer said, "Yes, I love the picture of you and Charlie on the wall."

Ben smiled and said, "Thank you, I am home for the long weekend."

Then Ben said, "Excuse me everyone, I have work to do."

Mr. Cason continued to check out the customers.

When the store was empty, he entered the storage room and said, "Ben, you don't have to work."

Ben smiled and said, "I want to. There are a few things that I see that need to be done. However, I need to leave at five o'clock today. I want to get home before Mom gets off work."

Mr. Cason said, "I am just glad that you are home. I missed you."

Ben said, "I missed you too. I brought you a gift."

Mr. Cason smiled and said, "That was very nice of you."

Ben gave Mr. Cason a t-shirt with the Middle Georgia State University logo on it.

Mr. Cason said, "I like it! Thanks!"

As Ben worked, he briefed Mr. Cason on everything that had happened during the last two weeks.

Mr. Cason said, "Ben, I'm so happy for you. Sounds like you have already established a reputation for yourself. You're doing good in your classes, and you are standing up for yourself with your friends. That's wonderful."

Ben said, "Yes, sir. I'm doing fine."

Mr. Cason said, "I can't believe you got those checks from those federal grants. That is wonderful. Continue to manage your money wisely. Make sure you don't let everyone know how much money you have. You want people to like you for you, not your money."

Ben said, "Yes sir, I still can't believe I received free grant money based on the fact that my family is poor."

Mr. Cason smiled and said, "That's just an example of God's favor. I believe, your best is yet to come."

Ben worked hard to get everything in order including cleaning the restroom and washing the trucks. Even though it had only been two weeks, he could see that Mr. Cason was not able to keep up with everything. It was the beginning of the month, so Ben completed all of the order forms for the month. He made an appointment with the golf course to make a delivery on Saturday.

After work, Ben rushed home to see his family. When he parked the truck in front of the house, David and Mary ran out of the door. They embraced and jumped up and down in a circle.

Ben said, "I missed you both."

Mary said, "We missed you too. It has only been two weeks, it seems like so much longer."

David said, "I'm glad you are home, I have so much to tell you."

Ben asked, "What are you cooking for dinner? It smells delicious. Did you cook enough for me?"

David said, "Yes, I did. I'm cooking spaghetti with meatballs again. I made the sauce from scratch."

Ben said, "I can't wait for dinner, I'm hungry. I worked at the golf shop this afternoon."

David asked, "How is Mr. Cason doing? I stopped by to say hello on last Saturday when I was in town purchasing supplies and he did not look good."

Ben said, "I noticed that he isn't looking good either. Looks like he is losing weight. He sounds good though."

David said, "Let's invite him over for dinner on Sunday."

Ben said, "That's a great idea. We can ask Mom if it is OK."

Mary said, "Ben, I have been taking Latin and I love it. Some of the students think it's hard, but I love it. So far I have the highest grade."

Ben said, "That's great. What do you like about it?"

Mary said, "I like learning the origins of words, the prefixes, and suffixes. If I don't know what a word means now, I can sometimes break it up and figure it out."

Ben said, "Wonderful! That is going to be very helpful when you take your SAT test."

Mary asked, "Is that the big test?"

Ben said, "Yes, if you plan to go to college, you have to score well on your SAT Test. Remember, I scored a 1495 out of 1600."

David said, "I'm scheduled to take mine next month."

Ben said, "The SAT test is a really big deal. How is Mom doing?"

David said, "She's doing good. She misses you, but overall she's fine."

Ben asked, "Has she said anything about her blood pressure?"

Mary said, "She went to the doctor last week. The doctor said that she was doing well for her to continue taking the medication. She no longer has to go to the drug store to get her pressure taken."

Ben said, "That's great."

Mary asked, "Ben, did you bring me anything?"

Ben laughed and said, "Yes, I did. I don't want to give it to you, until Mom comes home."

Ben enjoyed talking with his brother and sister. While sitting there, he realized how much he missed them. Time flew by, it was almost time for Mom to come home. They all piled in Ben's truck and drove to the rideshare.

When Mom got out of the car, she saw the truck. She beamed with pride. Holding back his tears, Ben hugged his mom. His Mom was so excited to see him. They all piled in the truck and drove home. As they entered the house, David rushed to the kitchen. Mom washed her hands and met everyone at the table. Mom was so happy to have all of her children at home. Ben said grace.

Mom started her inquisitions. This time she started with Ben.

She asked, "Ben, how is college? We got your letter last week, but fill us in on what has happened this week."

Ben said, "More of the same. The people at the tutoring center are very happy with my work. Miss Tiffany wants me to train all of the other tutors."

Surprised Mom said, "You've only been there two weeks and they want you to give a training session. That means you're doing a great job."

David asked, "Have you met any girls that you like?"

Ben said, "I have met many girls, but no one that I would like to be a close friend. Except Tammy, you remember the tour guide."

Mary said, "Yes, she was very nice."

Ben said, "She's a good friend. We have Calculus class together, so we study together at least once a week."

Mom said, "I liked Tammy when we met. She was very down to earth, very intelligent, and considerate."

Ben said, "Yes ma'am, she's a good friend."

Mary said, "She's white, so she can't be your girlfriend."

Mom said, "Mary, just because someone is another race does not mean that you can't have a relationship with them. However, it does make it difficult on a lot of levels. You all know the history about black men being lynched because they looked at a white woman. Yes, it's 1975 and some things have changed, but blacks are still not accepted as equals in everything. We all need to be mindful that everyone does not accept change, especially when it comes to interracial couples. We just all need to be aware."

Mom continued, "However, love does not know color. We love Mr. Cason and he's white."

Mary said, "Oh, I didn't think about that. You're right when I get older and start traveling. I may meet a Frenchman and fall in love."

Everyone laughed.

Mom said, "As long as that Frenchman loves God, loves you, and is good to you; that would be fine with me."

Ben said, "Mom, I have met people from all over the world already. I have one class with a guy from England. In my speech class, there's a girl from Brazil. I have to concentrate to understand her sometimes."

Mary laughed and said, "I can't wait to go to college."

David said, "Me too."

Mom said, "Slow down! Don't everyone try to leave me so fast. Mary, what's going on with you at school?"

Mary said, "Nothing out of the ordinary. My history teacher asked me if I wanted to participate in the History Fair."

Mom asked, "Do you?"

Mary said, "Not really, last year when I didn't win. I was sad."

Mom said, "Mary, your project was very good last year. We can't win every time."

Mary said flippantly, "I know. I'll think about it. I'm focused right now on improving my lexicon. I've been reading at least one book a week."

Ben said, "That's great Mary! The more you read, the better you'll be able to concentrate. It also improves your overall general knowledge of subjects. Keep it up!"

Mom asked, "David, how's that vocational cooking class going?"

David exclaimed, "It's great. Today, the principal announced that on Fridays we can open the culinary space up and sell sandwiches and other items to the other students."

Ben said, "Wow, that's great. So, you'll get experience running a restaurant."

David said, "Yes, each Friday, a different student will serve as the manager. I get to go first. So next Friday, I'll make all of the decisions about menu items and worker assignments. I'm excited."

Mom said, "That's impressive David. I'm sure you will do great. Who's in charge of teaching the class."

David said, "Remember, last year we were praying for Mrs. Smith from my middle school. She got promoted. She's in charge of the culinary program."

Mom said, "That's great. Well, I have some good news too."

Everyone put their fork down and stopped eating.

Mom said excitedly, "I got a promotion at work. I'm now the team leader for my section. My hours will stay the same, but I will get a pay increase of $1.75 an hour. Now I will be making $3.55 an hour!"

Ben said, "Mom, that's great news. I was worried about not working at Mr. Cason's and not being able to contribute to the family bills."

Mom said, "Ben, you don't have to worry. God continues to bless our family. So, don't you worry at all. Do you need any money?"

Ben said, "No ma'am. I have more than I need. I was thinking that you may need some. Can you believe I received checks for $2,700 in grant money this semester and will receive the same each semester that I'm in college?"

Mom said, "That's unbelievable! Did you deposit it in the bank?"

Ben said, "Yes ma'am"

Mom said, 'Look how God has blessed. I got a raise and Ben received grant money for anything he needs while he's at school. We can't help but praise God. Everyone hold hands while I pray. God, we come to you now so grateful for all that you are doing in our lives. You continue to provide for us abundantly each and every day. We know these financial blessings come from you. Please continue to give Ben traveling grace as he drives back and forth to school. Continue to order our steps and provide all that we need. In Jesus name we pray."

Everyone said, "Amen!"

Ben asked, "Mom, can we invite Mr. Cason to dinner on Sunday?"

Mom said, "That would be great. I saw him in town on Saturday, he looked like he lost a little weight."

Ben said, "I noticed that too."

Mom said, "David, this spaghetti sauce tastes different. It tastes better than the last time. Did you do something different?"

David said excitedly, "I'm so glad you noticed. I made the sauce from scratch this time."

Ben said, "It's delicious. The food in the cafeteria definitely does not taste like this."

Everyone laughed.

After dinner, Ben gave everyone a t-shirt with the Middle Georgia State University logo on. They all loved it.

The weekend flew by. Ben worked hard at the golf shop to complete as many tasks as he could. He had to be scrupulous. He did not want to leave anything undone. Everyone was happy to see Ben at church. He paid his tithes on the grant money he received. Mr. Cason enjoyed dinner on Sunday after work.

Mr. Cason said, "David, your cooking is getting better each week."

Mom said, "Yes, it is. I'm so proud of him."

Mary said, "Mr. Cason, you did not eat as much as you usually do."

Mr. Cason laughed and said, "Mary, you are very observant. You're right. I have been having a few problems. I have an appointment with the doctor on Tuesday. So hopefully he'll tell me what's going on."

Mom asked, "Do you need anything?"

Mr. Cason said, "No, I'm fine. I'm just not as hungry as I usually am."

Mary suggested, "Why don't you come to dinner on every Sunday."

Mom said, "That's a great idea. We would love that."

David said, "Then you can take some leftovers home. When you get hungry, you will have some good food."

Ben said, "I have also decided that I will come home every other weekend. That way, I can visit all of you who I miss terribly. I can also make sure everything is taken care of at the shop."

Mr. Cason said, "Well, how can I turn down such love. I would love to come to dinner every Sunday. I also love the idea of seeing Ben every other weekend."

4

WHAT A DIFFERENCE A SEMESTER MAKES!

Going home every other weekend was a great idea. Ben was able to see his family and keep the golf shop going. Mr. Cason was diagnosed with diabetes. The doctor prescribed medication. He was feeling much better. David adjusted his recipes to support Mr. Cason's diagnosis.

Ben enjoyed college. He liked living on his own, he liked learning different things, and he also enjoyed meeting different people. He continued to make friends, but Caleb and Joshua were his best friends.

It was time for finals, everyone was getting stressed. Ben was doing well in his classes, he had all A's. Not all of the A's were over the grade of ninety-five, but in Calculus he was just happy to still have an A.

For Christmas Break, he would have five weeks off from school. He was excited about that. Ben continued to pray for everything. It had been five months; Joshua's drinking was getting worse. Not only was he drinking at parties, he started drinking through the week. Joshua had been counseled by the dorm coordinator. The next time Mr. Clark saw him drunk, he was going to inform his parents.

Joshua said, "I don't know who Mr. Clark thinks he is. Why does it matter if I drink a little bit every now and then?"

Caleb said, "Man, it's more than every now and then. Your grades are falling. You don't want to study. You don't want to hang out anymore, unless it's a party."

Ben said, "Joshua, I have been praying or you. It seems the more I pray, the worse you get."

Joshua yelled, "Then stop praying!"

Ben said, "Joshua, you're only eighteen. You have your whole life ahead of you. Don't mess it up."

Joshua exclaimed, "Don't you think I know that. I don't want to drink anymore, but I can't stop. When I don't drink something, I feel horrible. Then when I drink something, I can't stop."

Caleb said sadly, "Joshua, we have to face facts; you're addicted."

Joshua said, "I know. How did this happen to me?"

Ben said, "I read an article the other day about alcoholism. It said that sometimes it's genetic. We all have genes that predispose us to different issues. That's why we need to know our family medical history."

Joshua said, "I know that too. My mother was an alcoholic when I was young. She went to Alcohol Anonymous and got clean. She has not drunk alcohol for ten years. I did not think it would happen to me."

Ben asked, "Have you talked to her about this?"

Joshua said, "I'm ashamed to talk about it."

Caleb suggested, "You'll be home for five weeks during the break. That will give you time."

Joshua said, "Well, I'm sober now. I better go study for these finals."

The tutoring center was not open during exam week, so Ben could study for his final exams. Final grades would be mailed to the student's home address.

Classes were chosen for the next semester. Ben was able to get somewhat of the same schedule. All of his classes would be over by eleven o'clock in the morning. He planned to continue volunteering at the Tutoring Center. Ben and Tammy continued to study Calculus together.

Ben asked, "Tammy, when do you plan to leave to go home for Christmas break?"

Tammy said, "All of my exams will be over by Wednesday; I plan to leave on Thursday. I will ride the bus home to Columbus."

Ben asked, "How far away is that?"

Tammy said, "Only about an hour and a half south west."

Ben asked, "Do you need a ride to the bus station?"

Tammy replied, "No, thank you. My roommate will drop be off."

Ben said, "Tammy, I haven't noticed you dating anyone."

Tammy said, "I had a boyfriend last year, but I found out he was cheating on me. So, we broke up."

Ben said, "I'm sorry to hear that."

Tammy said, "Don't be, I suspected it. I was just waiting on proof."

Ben asked, "What do you plan to do after college?"

Tammy replied, "I'm still not sure. I would not mind working for a large corporation. I also would like to start my own business."

Ben asked, "What type of business would you like to start?"

Tammy said, "I'm not sure about that either. I enjoy helping people. I love decorating. Possibly an event center that would help people with their celebrations or parties."

Ben said, "That sounds great."

Tammy said, "First, I need some experience and information. I signed up to take the Entrepreneurial Business class next semester. I am excited about that."

Ben said, "I saw that class, but I can't take it until my junior year. Do you still have your biology book?"

Tammy answered, "Yes, why?"

Ben said, "I think I may be able to pass the CLEP test for biology. I wanted to study a little over the Christmas break."

Tammy said, "That would be great. If you CLEP two more classes, you can graduate early. Instead of May 1979, you could graduate December 1978."

Ben agreed, "I was thinking the same thing."

Tammy inquired, "What other course are you thinking about?"

Ben said, "I'm pretty good in history, but I don't know. I may use the summer to study history."

Tammy said, "I still have my history book too. If you have time, we can walk to the dorm and get them?"

Ben said, "That would be great. Thanks Tammy!"

Tammy asked, "Were you able to get the Business Ethics class?"

Ben replied, "Yes! However, only the Tuesday/Thursday class was available. I have it at 9:30 am."

Tammy exclaimed, "That's the session I got too! We will have another class together."

Ben said, "That's great. I enjoy studying with you."

Tammy said, "Me too."

Ben completed his finals. He felt good about his grades. However, he did not feel that he aced the Calculus final. He did feel that he passed. His truck was packed and he was headed home to Fairville. While he was in Macon, he bought all of his Christmas gifts. He wanted to get his shopping out of the way. He knew that he would be working hard at the golf shop over the next five weeks. It would be early when he arrived in Fairville. He decided to go straight to the golf shop again. He parked his truck in the front of the store.

As he entered the shop, Mr. Cason was checking out a customer. It was Mr. Jerry Green. Mr. Cason interrupted his sale and rushed to hug Ben. Ben loved Mr. Cason's hugs. They were filled with so much love.

Mr. Cason exclaimed, "Welcome home Ben!"

Ben said, "I'm glad to be home."

Mr. Cason exclaimed, "Jerry, you remember Ben. Don't you?"

Jerry said, "Of course I do. Good to see you Ben. How is college?"

Ben replied, "I really like it sir. I am learning a lot and meeting a lot of different people."

Jerry said, "Everyone in this town is very proud of you, including me. Keep up the good work."

Ben said, "Thank you sir. I will."

Jerry left the store, Mr. Cason followed him to the door and waved goodbye.

Surprised Ben said, "Mr. Green was very nice."

Mr. Cason smiled and said, "I told you, this town was changing for the better."

Ben laughed.

Mr. Cason asked, "How do you think you did on your final exams?"

Ben said, "I think I did well. I'm just glad calculus is over. Professor Drucilla James did not play. It was truly challenging."

Mr. Cason asked, "Do you think you could tutor someone in it?

Ben laughed and said, "Possibly! However, I won't volunteer."

Mr. Cason said, "I'm just glad that you're home."

Ben said, "Mr. Cason, you look a lot better!"

Mr. Cason said, "I feel a lot better! I have been on the medication for diabetes for about three months now. I guess it's working. I have an appetite now, I have stopped losing weight. I'm not as tired as I was. So, I am doing better."

Ben said, "That's great. I have been praying for you."

Mr. Cason said, "Well, God heard your prayers. Keep it up!"

Ben worked in the shop until five o'clock. He wanted to get home to see his siblings. As Ben parked the truck in front of the house, Mary and David ran out. He could see that Mary was getting taller and David had started to grow a mustache.

Ben asked, "David, what's that stuff above your top lip?"

David exclaimed, "You can see it?"

Mary joked, "I still think he needs to wash his face, it's just dirt."

Everyone laughed.

Ben said, "Mary, you're getting taller."

Mary said, "I know, my feet have also grown. I can't wear my church shoes anymore and my school shoes are tight. Mom said we would go shopping on Saturday."

Ben said, "Well, I will be home for the next five weeks. I don't have to go back to school until January eleventh."

David said, "That's great. It will be like old times. I got my learners permit last month."

Ben said, "That's great, I'll give you driving lessons while I'm home."

Mary asked, "Will you be working at the golf shop every day."

Ben said, "Yes, I will. I plan to talk to Mr. Cason about closing the shop at least one day a week."

David said, "That's a good idea, I don't know how he works seven days a week."

Mary said, "It's probably because he doesn't have anything else to do."

Ben said, "I didn't think about that. You're probably right Mary."

David said, "For dinner we are having meat loaf, mashed potatoes, and green beans."

Ben said, "That sounds delicious. Let me go get cleaned up before Mom comes home."

When it was time they all piled into the truck to go to the rideshare to pick up Mom. Mom got out of her coworker's car and pointed at the truck. She was telling her coworker something. Mom beamed with pride as she walked to the truck. Mary took her work bag, Ben hugged his mother, and they all got in the truck and drove home.

Mom said, "Ben, you're going to spoil me by picking me up at the rideshare."

Ben said, "Mom, I love spoiling you!"

As everyone walked into the house, Mom said, "David, dinner smells amazing. Let me wash my hands and I will meet you all at the table."

David said grace. Mom started her inquisitions.

She asked, "Ben, how long will you be home?"

Ben answered, "Until January eleventh! The new semester starts on Monday the twelfth."

Mom asked, "Well, how are your grades?"

Ben said, "Final grades will be mailed home in about two weeks. I did well. I should have all A's, but I won't be surprised if I get a 'B' in Calculus."

Mom laughed and said, "Well, a B is not the end of the world, if it's the best that you can do."

Everyone laughed.

Mom said, "David, this meatloaf is delicious. What did you do?

David said proudly, "I added some buttery crackers and Worcestershire sauce for better texture and flavor."

Ben said, "David, this tastes better than Mom's meatloaf."

Mary said, "I still like your mashed potatoes."

David said, "I dropped the cheese to make it healthier. I just add garlic, salt, and pepper to the mashed potatoes now."

Mom said, "David, you're a great cook, inventive, and health conscious."

David said, "Thank you. I talked to Mr. Knowlton about culinary school in Atlanta. He told me that culinary schools accept federal grants and some have dormitories. Next year, he would help me complete my federal grant application. Ben, he also told me to remind you to stop by so you can do your federal grant application for the next school year."

Ben said, "Thanks for the reminder."

Mom asked, "So next year, you will apply to the culinary school in Atlanta?"

David said, "Yes, ma'am. I found out that I can go there and receive a certificate. The certificate will allow me to work at various restaurants or I can pursue a Bachelor of Science degree in Culinary Arts."

Mom asked, "Which do you want?"

David said, "I want to do more than work in a restaurant. I

want to someday own a place. So, I want to pursue the Bachelor of Science degree."

Mom said, "That sounds wonderful. I will continue to pray that God will bless your efforts."

David said, "The culinary school does not have academic scholarships like other universities, but they do have scholarships that I can apply for."

Mom said, "I'm not worried, God will provide."

Mary announced, "I have some good news. My Latin teacher said that I could apply for a summer program that's designed for high school students."

Mom asked, "You're not graduating early, are you?"

Everyone laughed.

Mary laughed and said, "No, but there is a program that I'm interested in for the summer. Middle Georgia State University has a summer program that teaches French and Spanish. It's a six-week program. The cost is $500, but that includes housing and meals. Of course, everyone that applies does not get accepted. My Latin teacher said that she will write me a great recommendation. Mom, I know $500 is a lot, but I want to apply."

Mom exclaimed, "Mary, you're talking about being gone for the summer, by then you will only be fourteen. I don't know."

Mary said, "Mom, I know, but other fourteen-year-olds will be there too."

Upset Mom said, "Mary, I have to pray about this. I have to find out more information about housing, supervision, and everything else. I know you want to experience the world, but the world is not always safe."

Mary said, "I understand. If not this Summer, maybe when I'm fifteen years old?"

Mom said loudly, "Mary, this is big! Let me pray about it before I say anything else."

Mary asked, "OK. Well, can you also pray about me going to a one-week Summer camp?"

Flustered Mom asked, "What summer camp?"

Mary said, "Well, Middle Georgia State University also offers a summer camp for youth ambassador training. You learn how to keep the environment clean. It's a combination of classroom and onsite learning. They tour a recycling center and a solar and wind powered facility."

Mom said, "That's more acceptable. How much is it?"

Mary replied, "It's sixty-five dollars for the week."

Mom said, "I can digest that. I will still pray and let you know."

Ben said, "Mary, you have big dreams, but you don't need to rush. The world will still be there when you're older."

Slouching in her chair Mary said, "I know. I just get excited."

Mom stood up and said, "I need to calm down. David, dinner was delicious. I'm going to sit on the porch!"

Everyone laughed.

5

CHRISTMAS CELEBRATION 1975

The days went by fast while working at the golf shop. Mary and David were out of school for the Christmas Break. David had orders for thirty cakes. He hired Mary to help him fill the orders. He would pay her one dollar for each cake that she helped him bake. Mr. Cason seemed to be doing well. He was full of energy. A letter from the university arrived indicating that Ben had received all A's. Yes, in Calculus his final grade was a ninety-one. Everyone was happy. Christmas was on a Thursday. Mr. Cason was coming to dinner as usual.

Mr. Cason suggested, "Ben, let's close the shop for Christmas break on the Wednesday before, Thursday, and Friday this year. We will open back up on Saturday after Christmas."

Ben asked, "OK, is anything wrong?"

Mr. Cason said, "No, nothing is wrong, I was just thinking I need to start taking some time off."

Ben said, "I think that's a great idea. You're currently open seven days a week. What do you think about closing the shop on Monday and Tuesday. On those days we have the least amount of sales."

Mr. Cason said, "That's a great idea. I will think about it."

Ben said, "We can also change the hours, so that you are only open from ten in the morning to five in the afternoon except on Sunday. Most of the customers come after lunch anyway. Very few customers come in after five o'clock."

Mr. Cason said, "That's a great observation. Look at you thinking like a businessman. I will think about that too."

Ben said, "I've completed all of my Christmas shopping, so I'm not sure what I will do on Wednesday, Christmas Eve."

Mr. Cason laughed and said, "Well, I have a doctor's appointment on that Wednesday. On the Friday after Christmas, I plan to sleep late."

Ben said, "Mr. Cason, I would love to go to your appointment with you."

Mr. Cason smiled and said, "I would like that."

Over the last few weeks, Ben had been importunate. He was able to get everything organized again. He felt good about the storage room, the display case, the orders were on track, and the inventory was updated. He had cleaned the windows, the restroom, and everything else that needed to be cleaned. The floor was mopped and waxed. He had dusted all of the display merchandise. The shop looked good. On Christmas Eve Ben drove Mr. Cason to his doctor's appointment.

While waiting in the waiting room Mr. Cason said, "Ben, I can't wait for you to meet my doctor, Dr. Little. I like him."

Ben smiled. The receptionist told Mr. Cason that the doctor was ready to see him. As Mr. Cason was walking into the examination room he stumbled.

Dr. Little said, "Hello Charlie! Have you stumbled like that before?"

Mr. Cason said, "Not really, but just then I could not feel my feet."

Dr. Little asked, "Can you climb up on the table?"

Mr. Cason laughed and said, "It is true that I am not as limber as I used to be, but I am not that old. Dr. Little, this is Ben Davis."

Dr. Little said, "Hello Ben, I feel like I already know you. How is college?"

Ben said, "It is fine sir. I enjoy it. I am glad that I am home for a little while."

After examining Mr. Cason's feet and legs, Dr. Little said, "Charlie, I see some swelling in your feet and ankles. You don't have feeling in some areas of your foot."

Mr. Cason said, "I am surprised, I have been feeling so much better since I started taking the medication."

Dr. Little said, "Well, there are some things we can do. I will write you an additional prescription, but I also want to run some more tests."

Mr. Cason said, "No problem."

Dr. Little asked, "Ben, how long will you be in town?"

Ben said, "I will be here until January eleventh."

Dr. Little said, "I want to schedule these tests right after Christmas. Would you be able to accompany Charlie?"

Ben said, "Yes sir."

Mr. Cason asked, "Doc, what do you think is wrong?"

Dr. Little said, "It can be a few things, but first I want to give you a diuretic to drain some of this fluid off of your feet. I will call you this afternoon with the appointment times for next week."

Mr. Cason smiled and said, "OK! Doc, I am not ready to leave this earth yet."

Dr. Little said, "I am not ready to let you go. I believe that we can correct these problems with some medication, so don't worry. I see that you are almost eighty-four years old; that is great."

Mr. Cason said, "Yes! I plan to be around at least three more years."

Dr. Little asked, "Why three?

Mr. Cason said, "I plan to see Ben graduate from college, then after that God can take me whenever he wants."

Dr. Little said, "That's a great plan."

Ben drove Mr. Cason home. Ben noticed that Mr. Cason's house was not as clean as he expected it to be.

Ben asked, "Mr. Cason, have you been cleaning your house yourself?"

Mr. Cason replied, "No, I had a cleaning lady. She died. I haven't found any one else that I trusted."

Ben said, "OK, on Friday my family and I will come over and give this house a good cleaning for you. Mom is off work until Monday."

Mr. Cason said, "That's alright. It's fine."

Ben exclaimed, "No sir, it is not. You can sleep late on Friday, but we will be here at ten o'clock in the morning to clean. It should not take us long."

Mr. Cason said, "I appreciate that Ben. I will see you tomorrow for dinner."

Ben asked, "Do you have something for dinner today?"

Mr. Cason replied, "Yes I do. I have a plate that David made me. All I have to do is warm it up in the oven."

Ben hugged Mr. Cason and said, "OK, I will see you tomorrow for dinner at three o'clock."

As Ben was walking out of the door, he felt sad. He did not want to leave Mr. Cason. He went home and told his family about what he had seen. Everyone agreed to clean Mr. Cason's house on Friday. It was Christmas Eve, everyone sat around the tree and talked while the radio played Christmas music in the background. Mom and David busied themselves in the kitchen. On Christmas morning, Mary was the first to get up as usual. When everyone gathered around the Christmas tree to read the Christmas Story, there was a sadness in the air.

Mom asked, "What's wrong?"

Mary said sadly, "I was just thinking about Mr. Cason. I don't want to open my gifts until he gets here."

David agreed, "Me neither."

Mom said, "That's fine. We can read the Christmas Story now and wait until he comes to open gifts. I see that there are a few gifts under the tree for him. So that's fine."

Everyone hugged Mom, then sat back down to listen to David read the Christmas Story. The family talked and busied themselves for the rest of the day. At exactly three o'clock there was a knock at the door.

Ben opened the door and happily said, "Merry Christmas Mr. Cason, come on in!"

Ben took the presents from the arms of Mr. Cason. Everyone hugged Mr. Cason and said Merry Christmas.

Mr. Cason said, "Merry Christmas everyone. I see that there are still gifts under the tree."

Mary exclaimed, "We decided to wait for you, then we all could open our gifts together."

Mr. Cason said, "That's so sweet. Thank you all. I would love to watch you open your gifts."

Everyone sat down to open gifts. Mary distributed all of the gifts to Mom first."

Mom said, "Wow, it seems like every year, I get more gifts."

Mary gave Mom her gift first. Mom tried to open the gift quickly, but everyone waited patiently.

Mom gasped and said, "Mary, this is beautiful. Where did you get this?"

Mom held up a blue crocheted blanket.

Mary said, "My friend, Becky, taught me to crochet. I only know how to do the granny square and single stitch. One day the Home Economics teacher was discarding yarn, I asked if I could have it? With all of the yarn, I made my Christmas gifts. Do you like it? I know that it is a small blanket."

Mom said, "It is beautiful. Mary. I have not seen you crocheting here at home."

Mary said, "I would crochet after school before you came home. I hid the yarn under our mattress."

Everyone laughed.

Mary passed out her gifts to everyone else. Mr. Cason opened his gift. It was a green crocheted blanket.

Mr. Cason said, "Mary, thank you so much. It is beautiful."

Mary smiled and said, "I picked green because you like golf."

Mr. Cason laughed and said, "I do like green. This is a very warm blanket. I love it."

Mary beamed with pride.

Ben and David opened their gifts. They each had blankets too.

Mary said, "I thought you could use them at the dorms to keep you warm."

Ben laughed and said, "Mary, this is so thoughtful, you're right. I did need a blanket, all I had was a bedspread. You used my college colors of purple, black, and grey. Mary, I love it."

David said, "Mary, I love it too. Are these the Atlanta Art Institute colors?

Mary said, "Yes, it was not easy finding those colors. I researched for a week. Finally, the librarian called the institute for me, and found out the school color is red. I thought that was kind of plain, so I put the 'Ai' on it in a darker red. Do you like it?

David said, "I love it. I really do."

Mr. Cason said, "OK, I will go next." He passed out all of his gifts.

Mary opened hers first, it was a book bag.

Confused, Mary held it up and asked, "What is this?"

Mr. Cason said, "They are not popular now, but one of my friends from Atlanta said, that this book bag is going to be the next big thing. You put your books in it and you can carry them on your back."

Mary said, "Oh!"

She stood up and put her arms through the straps. She modeled the book bag so all could see.

She said, "I like it. It leaves my hands free. Thank you, Mr. Cason! All of my books were getting heavy!"

David whined, "I want one."

Mr. Cason laughed and said, "Don't fret, I got you one too!"

Everyone laughed.

David opened his gift to find a red one.

Mr. Cason said, "I did not know that the Art Institute's color was red, just a happy coincidence."

David said, "I love it. Thank you, Mr. Cason."

Ben finally finished opening his gift. It was a purple book bag.

Ben said, "I know the other students are going to want one. Thank you, Mr. Cason. My books were getting heavy too."

Passing Ben, a smaller gift, Mr. Cason said, "I have one more for you Ben."

Ben smiled and opened the gift. It was a radio for his dorm room.

Ben said, "Thank you Mr. Cason, I was going to buy me one."

Mr. Cason laughed and said, "The other day when you were burnishing the display, you said, I need to get me a radio. So, I was trying to beat you to it."

Ben exclaimed, "Wow, this is not only a radio, but an alarm clock and a cassette player too. I can make my own mix tapes. I love it. I love it."

Mr. Cason smiled and said, "I'm glad."

Looking at Mom he said, "Phyllis, this is for you."

Mom said, "Thank you. I will try to open it quickly."

Mr. Cason said, "Take your time."

Everyone waited while Mom opened her gift. She looked at it and gasped.

She said, "Mr. Cason, this is the most beautiful thing I have ever seen."

She held up a necklace with three gemstones.

Mary said, "That's a beautiful necklace. Is it gold?"

Mr. Cason said, "Yes, it is. It's fourteen carat gold."

David asked, "What are those stones?"

Mom said, "These stones represent your birth months. The ruby is for July, when Ben was born. The emerald is for May, when David was born. The aquamarine is for March, when Mary was born."

Ben said, "At college, I heard some people talking about birthstones. I didn't know what they were talking about."

Mom said, "Mr. Cason, I will treasure this for the rest of my life. Thank you."

Everyone hugged Mr. Cason, he started to cry. He grabbed his handkerchief that was always in his pocket to wipe his eyes.

He said, "I truly enjoyed buying gifts for you all."

Mom said, "I will go next."

She passed out gifts to everyone. Mary opened hers first. It was a large pink diary with a lock and key. The diary was about eight inches by eleven inches in size. It was very large, usually diaries are four inches by eight inches in size.

Mary exclaimed, "Thank you Mom. I do have some thoughts and secrets that I wanted to write down. Becky talks about her diary all the time. I can't wait to show her mine. It's bigger than hers. I love it Mom."

Mom said, "There is something else in the box."

Looking confused, Mary pulled out an envelope.

Mom said, "Remember you asked if you could go away for the summer."

Mary was shifting her weight back and forth trying not to get excited.

Mom said, "After careful thought and prayer. I feel that you are still too young to go away. However, when you turn sixteen, I will be happy to let you go. Next Summer, Mr. Knowlton will be in charge of updating the middle school library with new books. He will need some helpers. He has agreed to hire you and Becky for six weeks during the summer. He'll pay you minimum wage for twenty-five hours a week. You and Becky can walk to the middle school together for work. The envelope is my promise that when you turn sixteen, I will help you find a camp to attend."

Mary jumped up and screamed, "I'll have a summer job in the library. I love it. I love it. I get to work with my best friend, Becky. Mom, I love it. I get to make money. I love it. I love it."

Reaching Mom, Mary hugged her tight and, "Mom, thank you."

Mom smiled and said, "You're responsible and mature enough to have a job at fourteen. I know this gift isn't anything fancy, but I figured you would like it."

Mr. Cason said, "Mary, you'll enjoy working."

Jumping up and down Mary said, "I'm so excited."

David finished opening his gift, he gasped, "Mom, you got me a Hibachi grill. I love it."

Mom said, "I saw it and thought of you."

David said, "We have one in the culinary classroom. All of the students love using it. I love it. Thanks, Mom. I can't wait to grill something."

Ben finished opening his gift, it was a new pair of shoes.

Ben exclaimed, "Look, I got some penny loafers. I love them."

Mom said, "I always want you to look your best. I noticed that your dress shoes were not looking as nice as I wanted them to."

Ben said, "Mom, I saw a lot of students wearing penny loafers at college. I really liked the way they looked. You can wear them with jeans or nice pants."

Mom said, "I'm glad you like them."

Ben said, "Mom, I do. You give such nice gifts."

Mom said, "My last gift is for you Mr. Cason."

Mr. Cason smiled and opened his gift. He was having a great time sharing presents with everyone. It was a bottle of cologne.

Mr. Cason said, "I really like this cologne. It smells good. Thank you, Phyllis, I needed some more cologne."

Mom said, "I thought so. Usually when I hug you, you smell so good. However lately, I had not smelled anything but soap."

Mr. Cason laughed and said, "You're right, I ran out and kept forgetting to purchase some more."

Mary said, "I like the way you smell Mr. Cason."

Mr. Cason laughed and said, "Thank you Mary. The last thing I want is to offend anyone with an effluvium."

Mary asked, "What does effluvium mean?"

Mr. Cason laughed and said, "I can't believe it. I know a word that you don't know. It means unpleasant odor."

Everyone laughed.

Passing out all of his gifts, David said, "I will go next."

Mary rushed to open her gift. It was a map of the world with stick pins.

David said, "I figured you could put it on the wall. Every time you visit somewhere new, you could put a pin in the map. Then it would be a visual for all the places you have traveled to."

Mary said, "I love it. I love it. Thanks, David."

Mr. Cason opened his gift. It was a hat.

David said, "I know you don't wear hats, but I thought this one would look nice on you."

Mr. Cason put the hat on his head; it was a flat cap.

Mom complimented, "Mr. Cason, that hat looks good on you."

Mary said, "It really does. I like it."

Mr. Cason said, "It feels good. I didn't realize that my head was cold."

Everyone laughed.

Mr. Cason said, "Thank you David."

Mom finally finished opening her gift.

She said, "David, this is a very nice apron, such good quality."

David said, "I got both of us aprons for when we're cooking together in the kitchen. I love cooking with you."

Mom smiled and said, "I love the apron! I love cooking with you too!"

Ben opened his gift from David; it was a spiraled, leather address book.

Ben said, "David, I really needed one of these. I'm meeting so many people at college and I want to keep in touch with them."

David said, "I thought the same thing. So, I got you and me one."

Everyone laughed.

Passing out his gifts, Ben said, "Well, I guess I'm the last one. I hope you like them."

Mary rushed to open her gift. It was a collection of socks in every color.

Mary gasped and said, "Ben, I love it. Some of these socks match my hair barrettes. I love it. There are stripes, polka dots, flowers, and solids. I love it. Thank you so much, Ben!"

Ben smiled and said, "I went to the Macon Mall and I asked a teenager what would be a great gift. She recommended the socks."

David finished opening his gift and said, "Ben, I can't believe you got me one of Julia Child's cookbooks. I'm not ready for that."

Mr. Cason said, "David, don't doubt yourself. I'm sure you can cook any of those recipes just as good as anyone else."

David exclaimed, "Well, I'm going to try!"

Everyone laughed.

Mom's gift was in a pretty bag, all she had to do was pull the drawstring.

Ben said, "I figured this would help you open your gift quickly, then you could reuse the gift bag again."

Everyone laughed.

Mom said, "I love that idea."

She pulled a medium size jewelry box out of the bag.

Ben said, "I didn't know Mr. Cason was getting you the necklace. I was thinking about all of your ear bobs and bracelets that you wear. This would be a nice place to keep them all."

Mom said, "This is a beautiful jewelry box."

As she opened the jewelry box, to her surprise it played music.

She gasped and said, "Listen! It's playing 'Amazing Grace.' Ben, I love it. Thank you so much."

Mary said, "I have read about music boxes before, but I have never seen one. It's beautiful."

Mr. Cason said, "Ben, that's a beautiful gift."

Mary said, "Mr. Cason, you still need to open your gift."

Mr. Cason finished opening his gift and saw a t-shirt that said 'Best Grandpa Ever!'

Mr. Cason could not stop crying. Ben hugged Mr. Cason and all of the family joined in.

Mr. Cason said, "I never thought I would be a grandpa since I didn't have any children. God has given me a daughter and three wonderful grandchildren. Ben, I love it. Thank you so much."

Everyone said, "We love you Mr. Cason!"

After dinner, everyone sat around the tree and talked until it was about ten o'clock. Mr. Cason left knowing that he would see his family tomorrow.

6

BIG DECISIONS

Early Friday morning, Mom was up cooking breakfast. Today, the family planned to clean Mr. Cason's house. Mom made sandwiches for lunch. She also packed the broom, mop, bucket, and cleaning supplies. Everyone piled in the truck and drove to Mr. Cason's house.

Mr. Cason lived in a very nice neighborhood. He had a large home. There were four bedrooms with two bathrooms. Mom made assignments while everyone was in the truck. She would clean the bathrooms. David would clean the kitchen. Mary would start in the living room and sweep the front porch. Ben would clean the bedrooms. When anyone finished their assigned area, they were to go help with the other bedrooms.

Mr. Cason happily opened the door and said, "Good morning everyone."

Everyone greeted Mr. Cason.

Smiling Mom said, "Mr. Cason, we have work to do, so we don't have time to chat."

Mr. Cason laughed while he moved out of the way. Mom walked around the house to get a general idea of what needed to be done. She was taken aback. It took all she had not to cry. The house was dusty, it smelled, and was not organized.

Mom asked, "Mr. Cason, when did your house keeper pass away?"

Mr. Cason said, "It has been a little while, I think it was last spring, maybe winter."

Mom said sternly, "Mr. Cason, we will clean this house today. However, when we leave today, you will be leaving with us. I don't want you to live alone anymore."

Mr. Cason said, "Phyllis, I'm fine."

Mom said, "No, you are not! I'm mad at myself for not asking you about this sooner. I saw a twin bed and a dresser in one of the bedrooms. We can take that to the house."

Mr. Cason tried to interrupt.

Putting her hand up Mom continued, "There will be no arguments. This is paramount. The boy's room has bunkbeds that we can stack again and we can put the twin bed on the other wall. I know that it's a small two-bedroom house, but we can make this work!"

Mr. Cason said, "Well, I will have to pay you for room and board."

Mom said, "Don't you insult me with trying to give me money. We love you. You are family and I would do the same for my mom or dad if either were alive."

Mary whined, "Mr. Cason, don't say no. I would love for you to live with us."

David said, "Me too."

Ben hugged Mr. Cason and everyone joined in. Mr. Cason could not refute.

He said, "Well, there are a few things that I would have to take with me."

Mom said, "Whatever you want is fine. Mary, after you

finish the living room, I want you to help Mr. Cason pack. Everyone else get to work!"

Everyone scattered.

Mr. Cason turned up the radio so everyone could listen to music while they worked. Everyone worked happily. Piles were created. There was a trash pile, a charity pile, and a pile of things that did not belong in the house.

After about three hours of work, Mom pulled out lunch. After lunch, the truck was loaded with the charity items, Ben went to drop them off. He made two trips. The trash cans overflowed, they were put on the street for pickup. The house looked so much better. A lot of the clutter was gone. It smelled clean. It was organized and ready to be lived in.

Trying not to cry Mr. Cason said, "This house has not looked this good since my wife died. Thank you so much."

Mom said, "No thanks is necessary. What things do you want to take to the house?"

Mr. Cason said, "I want to take my family pictures, some books, and the television. I also want to take my coffee maker. I think we should take all of the food in the house. We don't have to take it today, we can come back for it. I like oatmeal for breakfast, so I want to take my oatmeal today."

Mom laughed and said, "That's not a problem."

Looking at David she commanded, "David pack up the food."

David ran back to the kitchen.

Mary announced, "Mom, I helped Mr. Cason pack. The only thing that's left is his toiletries in the bathroom."

Mr. Cason said, "That won't take me long, I will be right back!"

Everyone scurried to pack the truck and Mr. Cason's car.

When Mr. Cason returned, he said, "David, Ben told me

that he's been teaching you how to drive. You want to drive my car home."

Embarrassed David said, "I'm not that good yet."

Mr. Cason said, "That's fine. It took your brother a little while to get the hang of it. I can give you lessons in the evening if you like."

David exclaimed, "That would be great!"

It was four o'clock when everyone left the house. Mr. Cason locked the door of his house. He felt good that it was clean again. However, he was ecstatic, that he was going to live with his family.

It took another hour or so to get the house set up for Mr. Cason. Ben and David stacked their bunk beds, deep cleaned the room, then put up the twin bed for Mr. Cason. There was enough space in the bedroom to put a straight chair for Mr. Cason to sit in.

Mary talked while she worked. She was very loquacious. She put sheets and a bedspread on the bed. At the foot of the bed she placed Mr. Cason's green blanket. She put his books and family pictures on the dresser next to his bed. She also unpacked Mr. Cason's clothes and put them in the dresser. He did not have any clothes that needed to be hung in the closet. Mom was busy setting up the kitchen. She made room for the coffee maker and put all of the food away.

The last thing retrieved from the truck was the television. Mr. Cason had a 25-inch color television console. It was a big piece of furniture. Mom took down the Christmas tree and made room for it in the living room. It was a little crowded, but it was OK.

Mr. Cason said, "Phyllis, I know this is an inconvenience, but I promise to be a good house guest."

Mom said lovingly, "Mr. Cason, you are not a guest. Remember, you are family."

Mr. Cason reached to get his handkerchief, then he said, "There are a few upgrades I would like to make."

Mom laughed and said, "Mr. Cason, you are free to do whatever you like."

It had been a long day. David prepared leftovers for dinner. Everyone watched television with Mr. Cason for a little while then went to bed. The next few days went by fast. Ben took Mr. Cason to his doctor's appointments. Dr. Little was happy to see all of the swelling gone from Mr. Cason's feet and ankles. He prescribed some additional medication and made a follow up appointment in three months.

While at the golf shop, Ben noticed that Mr. Cason was making a lot of phone calls. On the following Saturday, several deliveries were made to the house. Mr. Cason ordered a larger refrigerator and a shed for the back yard, where a new washer and dryer were installed. The Bell Company installed a telephone in the living room. Four window air conditioners were installed in the house. One was put in each bedroom, the living room, and the kitchen area.

Surprised Mom asked, "Mr. Cason, what have you done?"

Mr. Cason replied lovingly, "I'm just buying my daughter a few things that she needs."

Mom laughed and said, "Well, I guess I can't argue with that."

Mary asked, "Does this mean, we don't have to go to the laundry mat anymore?"

Mom smiled and said, "Yes, but you still have to do the laundry!"

After much deliberation Mr. Cason convinced Mom to let him buy all of the food and pay for the utility bills since he had installed so many appliances. Mom reluctantly gave in. Another week passed, it was time for Ben to go back to college. Everyone was sad again. But this time, it was not as bad. They knew that Ben would be home in two weeks.

As Ben drove his truck away from the house, he felt good. He was happy that Mr. Cason would be taken care of and he was elated that his mother did not have to go to laundry mat any more.

As he pulled into the parking lot of Martin Hall, part of him was glad to be back. He made some decisions. He was going to try and CLEP as many classes as he could. He would also talk to Dean Smith about other ways to help him graduate early. He knew that Mr. Cason was getting older. He wanted to make sure that he was at his graduation. As he was walking to his dorm room, Caleb was standing in the hallway.

Ben said, "Hi Caleb, is Joshua back yet?

Caleb said, "Mr. Clark just informed me that Joshua will not be coming back. He got in some trouble drinking during the break. His mother decided to keep him home. Joshua has enrolled in Alcoholics Anonymous and he plans to attend one of the junior colleges in Atlanta."

Ben said, "Wow, I didn't expect that."

Caleb said, "Mr. Clark gave me boxes. He asked me to pack up Joshua's belongings. His mom would come by to get his things sometime soon."

Ben said, "I'm speechless. I wanted Joshua to stop drinking, but I didn't want him to leave school. Do you need help packing?"

Caleb said sadly, "I really do. I'm sad, so I don't want to do it alone. Mr. Clark said that I would have the room to myself this semester."

Ben said, "Let me drop these things off in my room and I'll be right over to help."

Ben and Caleb packed all of Joshua's belongings. They took the boxes downstairs to Mr. Clark.

Ben asked, "Mr. Clark, does this happen often?"

Mr. Clark replied, "Unfortunately it does. We have several students that run into this problem or something similar each year. Students must make good decisions."

Caleb asked, "Is there any way that Ben and I can be roommates next year?"

Mr. Clark said, "Yes, you can. I will let the housing department know your requests."

Ben asked, "Will we still be assigned to Martin Hall?"

Mr. Clark said, "That depends on how many returning students request housing. Is that what you want?"

Caleb said, "I would like to stay here again. Wherever we are assigned, will be fine with me."

Ben said, "Me too!"

After class on Monday, Ben went to talk to Dean Smith.

Ben greeted, "Good afternoon Dean Smith."

Dean Smith said, "Good to see you Ben, I hope you had a great Christmas Break."

Ben said, "I did. I had not realized how much I missed my family."

Dean Smith asked, "Are you having any problems?"

Ben said, "No problems sir. I have decided that I want to graduate as early as possible. Earlier today, I passed the CLEP test for Biology. Miss Tiffany said that my score was high enough to CLEP both Biology I and Biology II."

Dean Smith said, "That is great. You are a very intelligent young man. Why do you want to graduate early?"

Ben said, "Mr. Cason is almost eighty-four years old. He

really wants to see me graduate from college and of course I want him there. However, I have to face facts that each year could be his last."

Sympathetically Dean Smith said, "Oh, I understand."

Ben said, "I think that I can CLEP History too. I plan to take the test when we come back in the fall. That will give me the summer to review."

Dean Smith said, "Counting the Biology score, you now have fifteen additional credit hours. That will allow you to graduate Dec 1978. You would need at least fifteen more credit hours to graduate May 1978. If you CLEP History I and History II that will give you six more credit hours. That would be the last class, you will be able to CLEP."

Ben said, "I was afraid of that. Do you have any suggestions?"

Dean Smith said, "Well, there is always summer school. How far away do you live?"

Ben replied, "I live in Fairville, about an hour and a half away."

Dean Smith asked, "Do you have transportation?"

Ben replied, "Yes sir, I do."

Dean Smith said, "Well, if you take three courses over the next two summers. That will set you up to graduate May 1978, a year early."

Ben asked, "Do summer courses meet like what I am use to now?"

Dean Smith said, "Most of them do. The Schedule of Classes has not been publicized for this summer yet. Usually it is available in April. We can meet again then to see what courses will be available for you to take. We don't want you to drive up here every day. I am sure we can find two classes that meet on the same day."

Ben said, "That would be great."

Dean Smith asked, "Do you plan to work during the summer?"

Ben replied, "Yes sir. I work at Mr. Cason's golf shop. I can figure out a schedule that I can do both."

Dean Smith said, "OK, we have a plan."

Hesitantly Ben asked, "One more question sir, will my scholarship pay for summer courses?"

Dean Smith said proudly, "Yes, it will."

Ben sighed and said, "I was a little worried about that."

Dean Smith smiled and said, "Son, it appears to me that all that you want will work out. You don't have to worry about a thing. Do you plan to volunteer at the Tutoring Center this semester?"

Ben said, "Yes sir, I do."

Dean Smith said, "I heard that you are doing good work over there. Keep it up."

Ben stood up and said, "Yes sir. Thank you for your help."

Dean Smith said, "Ben, it's a pleasure to help you. I wish more of my students were like you. Have a great day."

As Ben was leaving the Business building, he saw Tammy.

Enthusiastically Tammy said, "Ben, it's good to see you. Are you ready for class tomorrow?"

Ben said, "No, I was headed to purchase my textbooks before I volunteer."

Tammy said, "I picked up my books this morning, but I will walk over with you."

Walking Ben asked, "How was your Christmas Break?"

Tammy said, "It was good. My grandmother Iris gave me her car. So now I don't have to catch the bus anymore."

Ben said, "That's great. I've found that having transportation is a great benefit."

Tammy asked, "How was your Christmas break?"

Ben said, "It was great. Mr. Cason moved in with us."

Concerned Tammy asked, "Is he OK?"

Ben said, "Overall he is. He is almost eighty-four now, and my family did not like the idea of him living alone anymore. We love him."

Tammy said, "You have a very loving family, a lot of people would not do that."

Ben said, "Possibly not, but I was raised if you love someone then you take care of them."

Tammy said, "I like that!"

7

BEN AND TAMMY

Days turned into weeks. Weeks turned into months. The friendship between Caleb and Ben grew stronger. Classes were becoming more difficult, but Ben just studied a little harder. Ben and Tammy continued to study together. It was time for finals again.

Tammy said, "Ben, these last few months have flown by."

Ben said, "I know. I can't believe I have been in college for two semesters. Of course, I would love to keep an A average, but these courses are getting harder."

Tammy said, "I know, wait until next year. Let's try to get two classes together next year."

Ben said, "I would love that. What are you doing this summer?"

Tammy said, "Well, I can work again at the Visitor Center if I want. They are offering me forty hours a week for eight weeks. Last Summer I stayed with my cousin for two months during the summer. That option is open to me again if I want to work. What do you have planned?"

Ben said, "I will be working at the golf shop, but I will

also be taking two courses during the Summer. I will be taking Statistics and Financial Accounting on Tuesday and Thursday. The first class starts at 9:30, the second one starts at eleven o'clock."

Tammy exclaimed, "That is a lot."

Ben said, "I guess it is. I have to do it, if I want to graduate early. Since I have been going home every other weekend, I have the golf shop under control. It's not like I have to work hard to get it back in shape. It's at a point now where I can maintain. Of course, Mr. Cason still works there, but I try to lessen his responsibilities as much as I can. Anyway, I like working."

Tammy said, "Ben, you're the most dedicated person I've ever met."

Ben laughed and asked, "Is that a compliment?"

Tammy said, "Yes, it is. I'm very proud to call you friend."

Ben said, "If you decide to work this summer, maybe you can visit Fairville. My family would love to see you again."

Tammy said, "I would like that. I'll let you know."

Ben felt good about all of his final exams and was headed home. He had a two-week break before Summer classes started. When he arrived at the golf shop, Mr. Cason was checking out another customer. Business was booming!

As he entered the door, Mr. Cason said, "Ben, I'm so glad you are home!"

Ben smiled as he hugged Mr. Cason.

Mr. Cason said, "Jim, this is Ben Davis my grandson."

Jim said, "Ben, it is nice to meet you. Charlie talks about you, David, and Mary all the time. He is very proud of all of you."

Ben smiled and said, "We love him very much."

Jim said, "It is evident. Since he moved in with your family, he is so much happier. He looks great."

Mr. Cason exclaimed, "I feel great!"

Mr. Cason walked Jim to the door as he left the store. Ben went to check out the storage room.

Mr. Cason said, "Ben, I'm so glad you are home. Can you believe one year down, three more to go."

Ben said, "Mr. Cason, I hope it will only be two more years to go."

Obfuscated Mr. Cason said, "I don't understand."

Ben expounded, "I plan to take two courses during the summer. Those classes will be on Tuesday and Thursday for eight weeks. This will help me graduate in May 1978, so that's only two more years."

Mr. Cason said seriously, "I don't want you to take on too much now."

Ben said, "Well, since we are closed on Monday and Tuesday; I will only miss work on Thursday. I can work on Monday if I have too."

Mr. Cason said lovingly, "It's not about the work, I don't want you to put too much pressure on yourself to graduate early because you think I won't live until May 1979."

Ben said, "No sir, it's not that. I just want to have as much time with you as I can. So, the earlier I finish college, the sooner I will be able to come back and help you run the store."

Mr. Cason said seriously, "I'm not sure I like this new plan. Let's just see how the summer goes."

Reassuringly Ben said, "It will be fine. Tammy decided that she will be working this summer, I asked her to come visit Fairville and see you all."

Mr. Cason said, "I would like to see her again. It's nice that you are good friends."

Ben said, "Yes sir."

Mr. Cason asked, "Is that all?"

Ben said, "Yes sir. I don't think she sees me as a potential boyfriend. So, I'm happy just to be her friend."

Getting straight to the point, Mr. Cason asked, "Do you see her as a potential girlfriend?"

Ben said, "Well, I have met a lot of girls and none of them have impressed me as much as Tammy. She's very kind, intelligent, generous, considerate, and very pretty."

Mr. Cason said, "Ben, as much as I like Tammy, are you prepared for the social issues you will encounter if you go into a relationship with her?"

Ben said, "I thought about that. I think I could handle it. I'm just not sure if she would want to endure it."

Mr. Cason said, "Well, as you know times have changed. There are interracial couples all over the world. They are all over television; we have several couples here in Fairville."

Surprised Ben said, "Really, I didn't know that."

Mr. Cason said, "Yes, people around here are getting used to it. So, there is not as much unrest as it was last year."

Ben said, "Well, that's not an issue anyway for me. Like I said, I don't think Tammy is interested in me that way."

Mr. Cason said encouragingly, "Ben, you're a great catch! You're godly, a hard worker, good looking, extremely intelligent, dedicated, and loving. Don't be surprised if it has not crossed her mind."

Ben left work at five o'clock, Mr. Cason said that he would be home in time for dinner. Ben parked the truck, David and Mary ran out to see him. Ben hugged his siblings.

David reported, "My driving has improved and Mr. Cason is very proud of me."

Ben smiled and said, "That's great!"

David announced, "I have cake orders for the summer. I posted flyers all over town to advertise and I have gotten calls. So far, I have fifteen orders for May and twenty orders for June."

Ben said, "That's wonderful David. I'm so happy for you."

Mary said, "We get out of school for Summer on May twenty-eighth. I start working at the library on June seventh."

Ben said, "Wow, everyone will be working this summer."

Mary said, "I know. I have also been helping David cook. I'm pretty good. Right David?"

Smiling David agreed, "She's pretty good. I have learned a few things from her."

Ben asked, "Well, who is cooking today?"

As she ran in the house, Mary screamed, "David!"

Everyone laughed. Ben went alone to pick up his mother at the ride share. She was happy to see him. He told her his plans of taking some courses this summer.

Mom asked, "Ben, why are you taking courses?"

Ben said, "I want to graduate early. If I take two courses this summer and one course next summer, I can graduate May 1978 instead of May 1979."

Mom asked, "What is your rush?"

Ben said sadly, "I want to make sure that Mr. Cason is still alive when I graduate."

Mom said lovingly, "Ben, you don't have to worry about that. He's getting stronger every day."

Ben said, "I know, but I still think this is best."

Mom said, "God gives each of us intuition. I can't say what you feel is not true. If at any time, it gets too much, I want you to scale back and relax."

Ben said, "Yes ma'am."

As usual David cooked another wonderful dinner. He was

experimenting with different desserts. He always made a sugar free one for Mr. Cason because of his diabetes. After dinner, he presented eclairs.

Mom said, "David, I have never had an éclair before, but I like it."

Mary critiqued, "I think it needed some more sugar."

Mr. Cason said, "Well, the one he made for me is delicious" Everyone laughed.

The summer went by fast, everyone worked. Classes were going well. Statistics was an easy class, but Financial Accounting was challenging. Ben had lunch with Tammy every Tuesday and Thursday.

Tammy said, "Ben, the fourth of July is this weekend. Is your family doing anything special?"

Ben said, "Nothing special! Would you like to come visit?"

Tammy said, "That would be great. Maybe I could drive down on Friday after work and come back on Monday. I have Monday off because the fourth falls on Sunday."

Ben said, "That would be great. We have a small house, but we can make room for you."

Tammy asked, "Are you sure?"

Ben said, "Yes, my family is excited to see you again."

Tammy asked, "Can you write down directions for me."

Ben said, "Of course, I will give you directions to the golf shop. I will still be working on Friday by the time you get there."

Tammy said, "Great, I will see you around four o'clock tomorrow afternoon."

Ben rushed home to tell his family. They were excited about seeing Tammy.

Mom said, "Well, she can sleep in the bed with Mary. I will sleep here on the couch."

Ben asked, "Mom, are you sure?"

Mom said, "Yes, that will work. Did you tell her that we attend church on Sunday?"

Ben said, "Yes ma'am. She enjoys going to church."

On Friday, Tammy arrived at the golf shop at four o'clock. Mr. Cason was checking out a customer.

Mr. Cason greeted Tammy, "Tammy, it's wonderful to see you again. I will be right with you."

Tammy walked around the shop. Mr. Cason walked the customer to the door and waved goodbye. Mr. Cason turned to Tammy to give her a hug.

Tammy said, "Mr. Cason, this is a very nice shop."

Mr. Cason said proudly, "All of the credit goes to Ben. He has made this shop look better than it has ever looked. People think that he's under my tutelage, I am under his! He will be right back, he went to make a delivery to the golf course."

Tammy said, "That's fine."

Mr. Cason asked, "How was your drive?"

Tammy said, "It was very pleasurable. The weather is very nice here in Fairville. The zephyr is refreshing. Ben gave me great directions."

At that time Ben walked in from the storage room.

Ben laughed and asked, "Did I hear my name?"

Tammy and Mr. Cason laughed.

Ben said, "I'm glad that you did not have any problems finding the place."

Tammy said, "I really enjoyed the drive, it was very scenic and peaceful."

Mr. Cason said, "Ben, it's almost time to close up. Why don't you and Tammy walk around town for a little while."

Ben said, "That's a great idea. Tammy, do you feel like walking?"

Tammy said, "That sounds nice."

As they walked around town, they talked about everything. Ben told Tammy the history of the town and pointed out some historical spots. After the walk, Tammy followed Ben in her car to the house. As they drove up to the house, Mary and David ran out to greet them.

Mary hugged Tammy and said, "I'm so glad that you are here. We will be sharing a room together, is that OK?

Tammy said, "That sounds like fun."

David said, "Ben said that lasagna was one of your favorite meals, so I prepared that with a salad."

Tammy said, "That's really sweet. I heard that you are a good cook."

Mary asked, "Can you cook?"

Tammy said, "Yes I can, my Grandmother Iris taught me."

Mary said, "We won't have dinner until seven o'clock when Mom gets home. Can you wait until then?"

Tammy said, "No problem, I can wait."

David took Tammy's suitcase from Ben and took it in the house.

Ben laughed and said, "We're all very happy that you could come."

As they walked in the house Tammy said, "I am too. This is a nice neighborhood, it seems quiet."

Ben said, "Most of the time it is."

Everyone talked until it was time to go get Mom from the rideshare. Tammy rode in the truck with Ben while Mary and David stayed at the house.

When Mom saw the truck, she smiled and walked a little faster toward it. Ben hugged his mother, took her work bag, then opened the truck door for her to get in. As she got in the truck, she leaned over to hug Tammy.

Mom said, "Tammy, I'm so glad to see you again."

Tammy said, "I'm glad to see you too. Your family is so loving. I love that."

Mom said, "I guess you are right, we are very loving. We try to show love to everyone that we care about."

Tammy said, "My Grandmother Iris and mother are like that."

Mom asked, "What about your father?"

Tammy said, "He does not show his love in the same way."

Mom asked, "Do you have any siblings?"

Tammy said, "Yes ma'am, I have an older brother who lives in Atlanta."

Ben asked, "Do you see him often?"

Tammy said, "No, not much. He wants me to move to Atlanta when I graduate."

Mom asked, "Is that what you want to do?"

Tammy said, "I'm not sure. Of course, I will apply for some jobs in Atlanta. I'm not sure if I want to live in the big city."

Mom laughed and said, "I can understand that, Atlanta is not for everyone."

As Ben parked the truck, he rushed to the other side to open the door for his mother. Mary and David ran out of the house to greet Mom.

Mom saw that Mr. Cason was parking his car and said, "Well, I guess everyone is home. David, something smells good."

David said, "I made lasagna. This is my first time?"

Mom said, "I'm sure it will be delicious. Let me wash up and I will meet you all at the table."

Mary said, "Mr. Cason, you're just in time."

Mr. Cason laughed and said, "You know that I'm not going

to miss dinner. I have gained twelve pounds since I moved in six months ago."

Everyone laughed. Mary said grace. David served the food. Mom said, "Tammy, usually I go around the table for everyone to tell me what's new. Today, I will start with Mary."

Mary said, "I have great news. You know how I want to be a polyglot. I will be taking Spanish in the fall. Today when we were working in the library, I found a cassette player with tapes that teach you foreign languages. There were tapes for Spanish, French, and Italian. Mr. Knowlton said, that they were no longer used. So, he said I could have them. He also said, that learning a foreign language through tapes had proven not as effective. I also found some workbooks. So, I plan to use the work books in conjunction with the tapes to learn."

Mom said, "That's great. Which will you start learning first?"

Mary said, "I will start with Spanish, since I will be taking that in the fall."

Tammy said, "That's great Mary. I took Spanish in high school, but I don't remember much of it."

Mary said, "I read that immersion is the best teacher. I plan to speak it here at home to practice."

Ben said, "I remember very few words. I probably can read it better than I can speak it."

David said, "I just took it two years ago and I don't remember anything but Hola!"

Everyone laughed.

Mom asked, "David, what's going on with you?"

David said, "I have eight cake orders so far this month. My business is really taking off. Mrs. Smith, the Culinary instructor, told me that one of the grocery stores is thinking about letting me sell some cakes in their store."

Mr. Cason interjected, "David, that's really big. You may have to formally start a business and get a business license. I will make an appointment with Hank Jennings, my lawyer, so he can advise us."

Mom agreed, "Great idea. It's one thing to sell cakes out of your house to people, but when you sell them to stores for resale that is on another level."

David said, "I know. I never expected this."

Tammy asked, "David, do you plan to make a cake this weekend? I would love to taste one of your cakes."

David said, "Yes I do. I plan to bake a three-layer coconut cake tomorrow."

Mom said proudly, "His cakes are really delicious. They are moist, tender, and very flavorful."

Tammy said, "I can't wait. This lasagna is delicious. You said that this is your first time making it?"

David said, "I had three recipes that I reviewed. I took aspects of one, and some aspects of the other. I'm glad you like it."

Mary said, "I had lasagna at school before, it was dry. This is very good."

Patting his stomach Mr. Cason said, "Tammy, you see why I'm gaining weight."

Everyone laughed.

Mom asked, "Ben, how are your classes coming?"

Ben said, "They are fine. I'm doing well."

Tammy said, "I heard Dean Smith bragging on you today. The Statistics instructor told him that out of all of her students that you are the best. Dean Smith said that many of the professors that have taught you say the same thing."

Ben smiled and said, "Well, there are only ten students in the statistics class."

Everyone laughed.

Mom said, "Ben has always been a good student. One of his gifts is that he is able to understand and process information quickly."

Mr. Cason said, "That's true. It did not take long for him to catch on at the golf shop. Most things I only had to tell him once."

Mom asked, "Tammy, do you have anything interesting going on?"

Tammy said, "Yes ma'am I do. This will be my last year of college. I graduate next year in May. However, I have already been offered a job there in Macon. I'm not sure that I will take it, but it's nice to be offered."

Mom said, "That is wonderful. What is the job?

Tammy said, "It's an event planning place, the job would be Operations Coordinator. I would oversee all events and budgets."

Ben exclaimed, "That's great. You said that you wanted experience in the event planning business."

Tammy said, "Yes I did. However, the salary is not as much as I know I can get in other jobs."

Mr. Cason suggested, "People sometimes take positions for experience and then leave the position for more money."

Tammy said, "I did not think of that. Thanks Mr. Cason."

Mom asked, "Mr. Cason, is anything new going on at the store?"

Mr. Cason said, "Yes, it is. Ben suggested that I changed the hours of the store. I'm now open less hours, but I continue to do more business. Each year Ben has worked at the shop, profits have increased. Last year I noticed more customers from other cities. Now it seems like every day, I see more customers from out of town than I see local. It seems that everything that Ben touches is blessed."

Ben smiled.

Mom said, "I believe it, God's hand is on him."

Tammy said, "I believe it too. The tutoring center is thriving now since Ben started volunteering there. My first two years at the university, I didn't know anyone who went to the tutoring center. Now, in each of my classes, I hear students talking about the tutoring center."

David said, "Well, you can't deny that."

Mom said, "I have some good news too."

Everyone put their fork down to listen to Mom.

Mom exclaimed, "I passed my test for my learner's permit this morning."

Ben said, "That's wonderful."

Mom continued, "Mr. Cason said that he would teach me how to drive too."

Mary said, "I can't wait until I'm fifteen, so I can get my learner's permit and learn how to drive."

David said, "Mom, I did not know you were studying."

Mom said, "I didn't tell anyone, I wanted it to be a surprise."

Ben said, "Well, it is."

Mr. Cason said, "We can start lessons next week."

Mom said, "I'm a little nervous, but OK."

Mary said, "Mr. Cason, I have been thinking. If we think of you as our grandpa and you introduce us as your grandchildren. Then I don't think we should call you Mr. Cason anymore."

David said, "The same thing crossed my mind."

Mr. Cason asked, "What do you want to call me?"

Mary said, "Well, I know some people say grandfather, papa, or granddaddy."

Tammy said, "I have two grandfathers. I call one Grandpa Jack, and the other Grandpa Ken."

Ben suggested, "Since we only have one, how about just grandpa."

Mary said, "I like that!"

Mr. Cason pulled the handkerchief out that was always in his pocket to wipe his tears and said, "That would be fine."

Mom said, "I used to call my dad, Daddy. I think I will call you Dad."

David said, "That sounds good. What do you think Grandpa?"

Mr. Cason tried to clear his throat, then he said, "It's music to my ears."

The rest of the weekend went by fast. The family enjoyed Tammy and she enjoyed the family. Tammy even enjoyed church. It was a little different than her church, but she had a good time. The city had fireworks on Sunday night, everyone went to the city park to watch the display. It was finally Monday and Tammy had to go.

Tammy said, "This has been a delightful trip."

Mom said, "You're welcome to come back anytime."

Mary said, "I hope I didn't talk too much."

Tammy said reassuringly, "Mary, no you did not talk too much. I enjoyed sharing a room with you."

Mr. Cason said, "Tammy, it's been wonderful spending time with you."

David said, "I packed you some cake and lasagna for later."

Tammy hugged everyone. Ben walked her to her car.

Ben said, "Tammy, I'll see you tomorrow for lunch."

Tammy said, "Yes, I look forward to it. I really had a great time."

Ben said, "I did too. Tammy, I was thinking. Would you go out with me on a real date?"

Tammy smiled and said, "I would love too!"

Trying to conceal his excitement Ben said, "Great, I'll let you know the details tomorrow."

Ben hugged Tammy then opened her car door. She got in and waved goodbye to everyone.

8

GRADUATION SEASON

B en pondered what would be a memorable first date with Tammy. It was hard, they had lunch together all of the time. He finally decided to take her roller skating and to dinner.

After lunch on Tuesday, Ben said, "Tammy, I was thinking we could go roller skating and have dinner on Friday?"

Tammy exclaimed, "I love to roller skate. That sounds like fun."

Ben smiled and said, "I'm glad you like that idea! Is there anywhere special you would like to have dinner?

Tammy said, "Ben, I'm a simple girl. You don't have to do a lot to impress me. I enjoy spending time with you; so, wherever we eat will be fine."

Ben said, "There's a new fast food place called Chic-fil-a. I heard great things about it."

Tammy said, "I have too. I would love to go there."

Ben said, "Great, I have to go now. I need to get back to Fairville. I'll see you on Thursday."

Tammy said, "Ben, I would love for you to meet my family. Do you think you could go to Columbus with me one weekend?"

Ben smiled and said, "I would love to meet your family. Yes, just let me know when and I will go."

Ben drove back to Fairville on cloud nine. Tammy set up the visit home for the following weekend. She did not want to delay introducing Ben to her family.

The first date was very memorable. They had a great time. Tammy was a good roller-skater. Ben was excited about making the trip to Columbus. He worked hard during the week to make sure everything was taken care of at the golf shop. His family was happy that he was going to meet Tammy's family. Mom prayed that they would accept Ben and there would be no issues about him being black. During the car ride to Columbus, Ben and Tammy talked about everything.

Ben asked, "Tammy, have you told your family that I'm black?"

Tammy said, "Yes I have."

Ben asked, "Did you perceive any issues?"

Tammy said, "Not from my mother and grandmother, but my dad was quiet. My dad is always quiet. I have only had a few boyfriends. My dad was quiet about each one."

Ben laughed and said, "Deep down I'm not worried, I just wanted to be prepared."

Tammy said, "I'm not worried at all. Who could not like you Ben?"

Ben smiled and said, "People who won't take the time to get to know me!"

Tammy laughed and said, "I'm sure by the time we leave, my family will want to adopt you."

Ben laughed. As he parked the truck in the driveway, Ben saw a man standing on the porch.

Ben asked, "Is that your dad?"

Tammy said, "Yeah, that's him. Let me say a quick prayer."

Tammy prayed, then they got out of the truck.

She ran to hug her father and then she introduced him to Ben.

Ben said, "Good afternoon Mr. Kennedy."

Mr. Kennedy said, "It's nice to meet you Ben. Please come in and meet the family."

When Ben entered the door, there were six people waiting in the living room to meet him. He relaxed and said a silent prayer.

Surprised Tammy said, "Wow, everyone is here. Ben, this is my mom, her parents are my Grandmother Iris and my Grandpa Jack. These are my father's parents. This is my Grandmother Kate and Grandpa Ken, and this is my brother, Paul.

Ben shook the men's hands and said, "Hello everyone, it's very nice to meet you all."

Mrs. Kennedy said, "Welcome Ben, we're so happy to meet you too."

Grandmother Iris said lovingly, "We don't mean to bombard you. We all were just excited about meeting you and none of us wanted to wait."

Ben smiled.

Grandmother Kate said, "Ben, we prepared dinner, I hope you all did not eat on the road."

Ben said, "No ma'am, we did not."

Grandpa Jack said, "Well, let's go to the dining room."

Ben asked, "May I use your restroom to wash up first."

Paul said, "I will show you the restroom."

After Ben finished cleaning up, Paul was waiting in the hallway to guide him to the dining room.

Paul asked, "Are you OK?"

Ben smiled and said, "I'm fine. I'm glad to meet everyone."

As Ben walked into the dining room, Grandmother Iris said, "Ben, please sit here between me and Kate."

Ben took his seat. The table was filled with food. Grandpa Jack blessed the table. Ben waited for food to be passed to him.

Tammy's father, Mr. Kennedy said, "Ben, Tammy told us that you are going into your sophomore year."

Ben replied, "Yes, sir. I'm excited."

Mrs. Kennedy asked, "Ben, did your mother or father graduate from college?"

Ben said, "No ma'am. I am the first to attend college in my family. My younger brother, David will be graduating this year from high school and he plans to attend the Atlanta Institute of the Arts to study culinary."

Mr. Kennedy asked, "Ben, how does your family feel about Tammy being white. Did they not want you to date a black girl?"

Ben smiled and said, "My father died when I was ten. My mother believes that as long as the person I date loves God and is good to me, that everything else will fall into place."

Grandmother Iris leaned over to hug Ben and said, "Ben, I believe the same thing."

Paul asked, "Ben, have you dated many girls?"

Ben smiled and said, "No, Tammy is my first girlfriend. I have met many girls, but Tammy is the only one that I have wanted to be a close friend. Our friendship has led to us dating."

Tammy tried to say something.

Grandpa Jack interjected, "Tammy, it's obvious that you care a lot about Ben or you would not have brought him home."

Grandmother Iris said, "I agree. Ben, we are not trying to give you the third degree. We love our Tammy and only want the best for her."

Grandpa Ken asked, "Ben, where do you work?"

Ben replied, "I have worked for Cason Golf Shop for the last three years."

Paul asked, "Do you still work there while you are in college?"

Ben replied, "Yes, I go home every other weekend to check on my family and I work at the store. Mr. Cason is eighty-four years old, so I try to keep the shop in order for him."

Grandmother Iris said, "That's very noble of you."

Mr. Kennedy said, "I'm confused, I thought you worked at the Tutoring Center."

Ben said, "I volunteer at the tutoring center on Tuesday, Wednesday, and Thursday from one to four o'clock."

Grandmother Kate said, "Ben, you are a hard worker. I like that."

Mr. Kennedy asked, "What are your grades like?"

Ben said, "So far I have a 4.0; Tammy has warned me that the upcoming courses will be challenging."

Mrs. Kennedy said, "Ben, that's quite impressive. You work, volunteer, and have good grades. Do you ever have any fun?"

Ben laughed and said, "Yes ma'am, my best friend is Caleb. We have fun. I don't like going to fraternity parties, but I enjoy movies, arcades, roller skating, bowling, and paddle boating, I like a lot of fun things."

Tammy was able to make eye contact with Ben, she smiled. Dinner was finally over.

Grandpa Jack said, "Ben, please join us outside."

Ben stood up and said, "Dinner was delicious. Thank you." He then followed all of the men outside.

Grandpa Jack said, "Ben, you seem like a nice young man."

Ben smiled.

Mr. Kennedy asked, "What attracted you to Tammy?"

Ben said, "My family met Tammy in June 1975. She gave us

the tour of the university campus. Last fall, surprisingly we had Calculus together. We became study partners. That's how our friendship started. She impressed me with her intelligence, her generosity, compassion, and work ethic. I also think that she is a beautiful girl. It was only this summer that I got up enough nerve to ask her on a date."

Paul said, "Ben, I know you have been bombarded with questions, but you are handling yourself well."

Ben smiled.

Grandpa Ken asked, "Ben, how do you feel about Tammy being older than you?"

Ben said, "I really have no feeling about that. Yes, she is about fifteen months older than me, but I don't see that as a problem."

Grandpa Jack asked, "When she graduates from college, you will still have two years to go."

Ben said, "No sir, I will graduate one year behind her. I was able to CLEP a few courses and I went to summer school this year. So, I only have to take one more course next summer, then I will be able to graduate May 1978."

Mr. Kennedy said, "Ben, you have proven yourself to be not only intelligent, but a very hard worker. You're dedicated, goal oriented, and a family man."

Ben said, "Yes sir."

Mr. Kennedy said, "I have no more questions for Ben. Does anyone else have any?"

Leaning forward Grandpa Jack asked, "Why did you not go into the military?"

Ben said, "I am not against the military, but I was able to get a full scholarship to Middle Georgia State University. I decided to take that path instead."

Paul said, "I did not know that you were on scholarship."

Ben said, "My family could not afford to pay for me to go to college, so my only option was to work hard to receive a scholarship."

Grandpa Jack asked, "Ben, have you registered to vote?"

Ben said, "Yes sir. I'm very excited about voting in the upcoming Presidential Election."

Grandpa Ken said, "Well Ben, you are a very impressive young man. All I ask is that you treat Tammy with love and respect."

Ben said, "Yes sir. I plan to."

Tammy's mother, Mrs. Kennedy, walked outside and asked, "Are you all finished with Ben?"

Mr. Kennedy smiled and said, "Yes, we are?"

Mrs. Kennedy said, "Well, we want to talk to him in the living room."

Ben got up and followed Mrs. Kennedy to the living room. Grandmother Kate and Grandmother Iris were waiting. Ben took a seat.

Mrs. Kennedy said, "Ben, Tammy has not brought any boys home from college to meet us."

Ben said, "I did not know that."

Grandmother Iris said, "So, we were all excited to meet you."

Ben smiled.

Grandmother Kate said, "Ben, you have been here about two hours already and you don't seem nervous."

Ben smiled and said, "I'm glad that you were not able to tell."

Mrs. Kennedy asked, "Do you plan to work at the golf shop after college."

Ben replied, "Right now I do. Mr. Cason has been very good to me and my family. As I said before, he is eighty-four now, so I can't imagine leaving him to work somewhere else."

Grandmother Kate said, "I thought you worked for your grandfather."

Ben smiled and said, "In a way I do. I don't know if Mr. Cason adopted my family or my family adopted Mr. Cason. Either way, we consider him family. My brother, sister, and I call him Grandpa. My mother calls him Dad. He lives with us now."

Mrs. Kennedy asked, "What about your other grandparents."

Ben said, "Unfortunately, they all died when I was very young."

Grandmother Iris said, "It's obvious that your loving disposition comes from being raised in a loving home."

Ben said proudly, "Yes ma'am, my mother is very loving. I was raised in church. I guess that is why I am who I am today."

Mr. Kennedy said, "I'm happy that you and Tammy are dating. You make a very nice couple."

Ben said, "Thank you!"

At that time Tammy walked into the room and asked, "Are you all finished with Ben now?"

Grandmother Iris said, "Yes, we are."

Tammy asked, "Ben, would you like to go for a walk in the neighborhood."

Ben said, "I would like that."

Ben stood up and said, "Excuse me ladies, it has been a pleasure talking to you."

Ben and Tammy left the house. The men came back in the living room.

Mr. Kennedy said, "I tried very hard to find something wrong with him."

Mrs. Kennedy said, "I know, I was searching hard too. He's a very nice young man."

Grandmother Iris said, "I'm impressed that he's a godly

man, he loves his family and God, which means he will treat Tammy right."

Paul said, "I have a few black friends in Atlanta, but none like him. I want him to be my friend!"

Everyone laughed.

Grandpa Jack said, "We put him under a lot a pressure today. He did not flinch. I know that an interracial relationship will be stressful, but he seems like he could handle it."

Grandpa Ken laughed and said, "I would have left, if I had walked into a room with all of us in it."

Paul said, "At first I felt sorry for him. After I saw how composed he was, I started feeling sorry for us."

Everyone laughed.

Mrs. Kennedy said, "Well, it's not like they are getting married. They are only dating."

Grandpa Ken said, "Tammy would be a fool to let that one get away."

Everyone laughed.

The rest of the weekend was great. Mr. Kennedy grilled on Saturday. Everyone attended church on Sunday. Ben enjoyed the service it was not as dynamic as his church. The sermon was very good. It was finally Sunday, time for Ben and Tammy to leave. Everyone hugged them goodbye and encouraged Ben to come back again soon.

Ben said, "I look forward to it."

After Tammy hugged all of her family, Ben opened her truck door to let her in. Everyone waved as they drove down the street.

Tammy said, "I told you there was nothing to worry about. My family really liked you. My brother told me to give you his phone number."

Ben said, "I had a great time. I liked them too."

The rest of year went by fast. Ben was able to CLEP both history courses. He made several trips back to Columbus and Tammy made several trips to Fairville. Tammy decided to accept the position at the event planning company. She was able to negotiate a higher salary. Even though the salary was not as high as she would have liked, it was much better than the initial offer.

Graduation season was quickly approaching. Tammy's graduation ceremony was scheduled for May 7, 1977. David's high school graduation ceremony was scheduled for May 21, 1977.

David was accepted into Atlanta's Institute of Art's Culinary program. He received a full scholarship that included tuition, fees, books, and housing. Everyone was very proud.

David was ranked fifth in his class. He was selected to do the prayer just like Ben. The family was very proud of him. Before his graduation, the family planned to attend Tammy's graduation. This was a chance for both families to meet. The graduation ceremony was scheduled for one o'clock on Saturday afternoon, so Tammy's family arrived in Macon on Friday afternoon.

Tammy coordinated a dinner for both families at one of the event planning venues. The dinner was scheduled for six o'clock. David drove the family up in Grandpa's car. Tammy's family had arrived earlier and checked into a hotel for the night. Everyone was finally at the dinner. Tammy bought outfits that she and Ben would wear. Their school colors were purple, grey, and black. Tammy wore a purple and grey dress. Ben wore a purple dress shirt with grey pants.

Everyone talked about what a cute couple they were. The dinner was delicious and the families got along well. Grandpa took pictures of everyone. He asked the waitress to take a photo of the group. No one wanted to leave.

On graduation day, everyone sat together to support Tammy. She graduated with honors. There were 985 graduates in her class. It was a beautiful ceremony. After the ceremony, everyone helped Tammy moved her things into her new apartment. Tammy served spaghetti and a salad to everyone. David made a cake to celebrate. Everyone sat around the apartment and talked until it was late.

Mom said, "Tammy, it's been a pleasure, but we need to head back to Fairville; we have church tomorrow morning." Everyone hugged each other, exchanged telephone numbers, addresses, and planned to get together soon.

The next few weeks were a blur. Soon it was time for David to graduate. Tammy attended the ceremony with the family. David spoke beautifully. His prayer was heartfelt and he received a standing ovation. The family and the community were very proud of him. Grandpa took pictures of everything.

When they finally got home, Mary said, "Wow, I can't believe David has graduated. It seems like the other day we were at Ben's graduation."

Mom said, "You're right, you will be in the tenth grade this fall, so in three years we will be right back here again."

Grandpa said, "Can you believe it, next year we will be going to Ben's college graduation?"

Ben said, "I know, these last two years have gone by fast."

The summer went by even faster. In July David planned a tour of Atlanta Institute of the Arts. Tammy wanted to go. So, David drove Grandpa's car and Ben drove his truck. The trip was a little over two hours.

David checked in. The tour guide welcomed everyone. The institute was very large. There were approximately 3,000 students currently enrolled. In the culinary department, there were 900 students. The Institute did not have a dormitory.

However, there were furnished apartments right next door, that were leased to students.

The family toured the campus and the apartments. David was very excited. Atlanta was a different world.

Grandpa asked. "Can freshmen have vehicles?"

The tour guide said, "Yes, but parking is an issue. There would be parking fees, if you parked in a nearby garage that was about one block away. Those fees were not paid by the Institute."

Grandpa said, "David, I have that other truck if you would like it as your graduation gift."

David said, "Thanks Grandpa. I would love it. If it gets too hectic to have a vehicle here, I can just leave it home and catch the bus back."

Grandpa said, "That would be fine."

David could see that Grandpa was getting tired.

David said, "This has been a great tour, thank you very much."

The tour guide asked, "Does anyone have any questions?"

Everyone was quiet, even Mary.

Tammy's brother Paul met the family at a popular restaurant near the Institute called *Gus's Fried Chicken*. Everyone had a great time and enjoyed their meal. Finally, it was time to head back to Fairville. It was hectic driving in Atlanta, but Ben and David were able to maneuver the vehicles well.

When the family finally arrived home, Mr. Cason said, "It has been a long day for me. Good night everyone."

Mom said, "Me too, that traffic wore me out."

David said, "That is something that I will definitely have to get used to."

Ben and Tammy sat outside on the porch and talked before turning in.

Tammy said, "Ben, this last year has been one of the best years of my life, and part of it is because of you."

Ben smiled and said, "I feel the same way. I thought I was happy before we started dating, but sometimes I feel guilty that I am so happy. I can't stop smiling."

Tammy said, "I'm so glad our families get along. Paul said that he had a great time at the restaurant today."

Ben said, "I really like your brother. He told me that he could get tickets to the Earth, Wind, and Fire concert next month. He wanted to know if we wanted to go with him."

Tammy said, "That would be great."

Ben said, "I know you have to leave early tomorrow, but I will see you on Monday for lunch."

Tammy leaned over to put her head on Ben's shoulder and said, "I don't want to go. It's getting harder to leave you."

Ben hugged her and said, "I know. The only way I have been able to deal with it, is to focus on the next time I will see you."

Tammy stood up and said, "I know Mary has a lot to talk about, so let me go to bed!"

Ben laughed and said, "You know my sister well."

9

TRAGEDY STRIKES

The next few weeks flew by. David prepared to leave for the Art Institute and Ben prepared to head back to Macon for his senior year of college. Since Tammy was working in Macon, they planned to have dinner together as much as possible. Ben would continue volunteering at the Tutoring Center. Caleb and Ben were still roommates.

Tammy said, "Ben, I plan to drive to Columbus on Wednesday. I need to drop off my parent's anniversary gift, since I won't be able to go home for the celebration."

Ben asked, "If you wait until Friday, I can drive down with you?"

Tammy said, "No, that's OK, I have an event on Sunday, so if I go now, I can spend a few days."

Ben asked "When will you be back?"

Tammy said, "I will be back on Saturday afternoon. Would you like to go to a movie on Saturday night? I heard good things about Star Wars!"

Ben said, "That would be great. Let me check your car before you go."

Tammy said, "I think it's fine."

Ben said, "Grandpa told me to always check the fluid levels and tire pressure before you make a trip."

Tammy laughed and said, "Ben, you're spoiling me."

Ben said, "I spoil people that I love."

Tammy said, "I guess I better get used to it."

Ben laughed and said, "I guess so"

As Ben was walking away, Tammy said, "Ben, I love you too!"

Ben smiled and said, "I'm glad."

On Wednesday, Tammy left early for her one-and-a-half-hour drive to Columbus. As she was driving on Highway 96 through some small towns right outside of Columbus. She stopped at the traffic light. When the light turned green, she drove off. Out of nowhere a driver ran the red light and crashed right into her car. Late that night, Mr. Kennedy received a call from the Georgia State Patrol. The patrolman reported that there had been an accident and Tammy Kennedy was in the car.

Shocked Mr. Kennedy asked, "Is Tammy alright?"

The patrolman said, "Sir, I am sorry to report that she did not make it. A drunk driver crashed into her car traveling at a high speed."

Mr. Kennedy dropped the phone. Mrs. Kennedy picked up the phone and told the patrolman who she was. The patrolman repeated his message and asked if they could come to the Piedmont Regional Hospital in Columbus to identify the body. Mrs. Kennedy was able to hang up the phone, then she broke down and cried.

After they identified the body, they called Ben's dorm. The dorm coordinator went to go get Ben. It was hard for Ben to understand the news through their tears. Ben was speechless.

Mrs. Kennedy asked, "Ben, are you still there?"

Ben said, "Yes, ma'am. I am sorry. I can't talk right now. I will drive to Columbus early tomorrow morning."

Ben could not think, he was overcome with grief. After about two hours, he was able to call home and inform Mom and Grandpa of the news.

Grandpa said, "Ben, I am so sorry! I can't talk right now."

Mom took the phone and said, "Ben, I know this is heartbreaking. My heart is broken too."

Ben heard Grandpa tell Mary in the background. He heard Mary crying.

Ben said, "Mom, tomorrow I will drive to Columbus."

Mom said, "OK. Call me when you get there. I will be in prayer for us all."

The next morning Ben left early. He cried for the entire drive. As he pulled up to the house, Mr. Kennedy was sitting on the porch. When he hugged Mr. Kennedy, he could not hold back his tears. Mr. Kennedy cried with him.

Mrs. Kennedy and all of the grandparents were sitting in the living room. Ben wiped his face and tried to appear strong, but it was not easy. They all hugged him. He could not stop crying.

Grandmother Iris said, 'Ben, this is the most difficult thing I have ever experience."

Grandmother Kate said, "Me too."

Mrs. Kennedy said, "We have to go to the funeral home tomorrow. Would you like to go with us?"

Ben said, "Yes ma'am. May I stay here at the house?"

Mr. Kennedy said, "Of course you can. Paul will be home later today."

Ben said, "Tammy was coming home to bring your anniversary gifts. We bought them, when we went shopping last week. She did not want to ship them because they were fragile."

Mr. Kennedy said, "I know, she was so excited about it. She told us that we would love them."

Ben said, "I have prayed so much my mouth is tired. I need God to help me, because I can't go on like this."

Grandpa Ken said, "Son, he has to help us all."

Funeral arrangements were made. The service would be held on Saturday. David was driving down from Atlanta, Mom would drive Grandpa and Mary down on Friday night. Ben reserved adjoining hotel rooms for his family.

On Saturday at the funeral, the church was filled with people, family, and friends that knew and loved Tammy. The ceremony was quick. Tammy was buried in the church cemetery. There was a repass in the church fellowship hall. Ben was numb. He could not imagine what his future would look like.

Grandpa said, "When my wife passed away, it took me a little while to start to live again."

Ben said, "I'm trying not to be angry with God. I know that he does not make mistakes. I don't understand why he would take her away from me when we were so happy."

Mom said, "I felt the same way when your dad died. I could not understand how I could go on and provide for three children by myself. Each day God gave me strength. It took me a long time to stop crying, but one day I stopped. I had three children that were relying on me. I had to pull myself together. I still think about your dad, but now I don't cry. I remember the good times that we shared. I'm thankful for those good times."

Ben said, "I am too. I loved Tammy, I had planned to ask her to marry me when I graduated next year."

Grandpa said sadly, "I know."

Mary said, "She was like a sister to me. I loved her so much."

David said, "I have been trying to pull myself together, but it's not easy."

Grandpa said, "We just have to take it one day at a time."

Everyone hugged Tammy's family and said they would stop by the house on Sunday before they left town. Ben spent the night at Tammy's parent's house. There was a gloom in the house.

Ben said, "Let's talk about some of the good times we had with Tammy."

Mrs. Kennedy said, "I'll start. Tammy was a beautiful baby. She was so pretty, this photographer tried to get us to let him take pictures of her."

Mr. Kennedy said, "I remember that! Why didn't we let him take pictures of her?"

Mrs. Kennedy laughed and said, "He looked like a hippie and we didn't believe he was a photographer."

Everyone laughed.

Mr. Kennedy said, "Oh, I remember. He turned out to be a famous photographer that went on to work for Cosmopolitan magazine."

Everyone laughed.

Grandma Iris said, "When Tammy was about nine years old, she used to follow me around the kitchen. She whined until I taught her how to cook. The first thing she learned to cook was scrambled eggs. She cooked scrambled eggs every time she came over to the house for a month."

Everyone talked about Tammy until there were no more tears. Laughter filled the house.

Ben said, "I plan to leave tomorrow, but I will come back to see you soon."

Mr. Kennedy said, "We would love that."

Grandpa Ken said, "Please let us know when your graduation is, we plan to be there."

Ben said, "I would love that."

As Ben drove back to the university, he tried to reason in his head why God would take Tammy from him. He decided to declare a three-day fast. He needed strength that only God could give to go through this ordeal. He checked in with his instructors to see what assignments he had missed.

When he stopped by the Tutoring Center, Miss Tiffany asked, "Ben, do you need to take some more time off from the Tutoring Center?"

Ben said, "No ma'am. I need to keep myself busy."

Miss Tiffany said, "There is a grief counselor on campus if you need to talk to someone."

Ben said, "No ma'am, right now I am OK. Thanks for the information."

Staying busy helped Ben deal with Tammy's death. On Thursday, Ben and Caleb planned to pack up Tammy's belongings and clear out her apartment.

Caleb said, "Ben, tomorrow is Thursday. Do you still want to pack Tammy's things?"

Ben said, "Yes, I do. Her parents told me to donate all of her furniture and her clothing. The only thing they wanted were her keepsakes like photos, degrees, etc. Goodwill is scheduled to pick up the furniture on Friday morning at eight o'clock."

Caleb asked, "Do you have boxes?"

Ben said, "Yes, I have everything we need at the apartment already."

Caleb said, "Ben, I know this is very hard for you. I think, you are handling it very well."

Ben said, "I'm trying, I am all cried out. So, there are no

more tears. I declared a fast and I think that helped me. I feel a little stronger, I feel like I am able to go on."

Caleb said, "I thought fasts were only for Lent during Easter time."

Ben said, "No, you can declare a fast at any time. When you give up certain things like food, habits, or anything that is distracting you from hearing God speak to you. You are able to get closer to God to gain strength and a better understanding about things."

Packing up Tammy's belonging was harder than he expected. Caleb helped him focus on the good times with Tammy. They reminisced and laughed. Ben saved many of the photos for himself. He kept a few of her dresses for Mary. He planned to make a trip next weekend to take Tammy's things to Columbus.

On Friday afternoon, he headed home. When he arrived at the golf shop, he noticed that it was closed. There was a sign on the door that said, 'Be right back.' Ben unlocked the store and started to work. Shortly after Grandpa returned.

Grandpa said, "Hi, Ben, I'm glad you are home. How are you doing?"

Ben said, "I'm better."

Grandpa hugged Ben. Ben was determined not to cry.

Ben asked, "Are you OK?"

Grandpa said, "Of course, it has been hard, but I'm doing better too."

Ben said, "There is a delivery scheduled for the golf course tomorrow."

Grandpa said, "I know. I am glad you are here. I need you to go with me to the Chevrolet dealership."

Ben asked, "You bought a new truck for the shop?"

Grandpa said, "Sort of! I bought a van this time. I also

bought a new car. The other car was starting to have problems. I didn't want Phyllis driving it and getting stranded somewhere."

Ben smiled and said, "Grandpa, you're always thinking of others. I thought you were a FORD man!"

Grandpa laughed and said, "I was, but Chevrolet gave me a better deal."

Ben laughed.

Grandpa asked, "How is your truck doing? Does it need any work?"

Ben said, "No sir, I have not had any problems with it at all? I had the oil changed last week."

Grandpa said, "Great. When cars start to give you problems, you always need to get them fixed. If they can't be fixed, then it's time to get rid of them."

Ben asked, "Grandpa, how long after your wife died did it take for you to feel normal again?"

Grandpa said, "We had been married for forty years. It was a long time. I was able to function, but there was a void. Truthfully, it was not until you came to work at the shop that the void was filled. I guess when I started to love again, the void started to close."

Ben said, "I don't think, I will ever love anyone else."

Grandpa said compassionately, "You are still so very young. God has another woman for you. One that will bring you just as much joy as Tammy did, maybe more."

Ben said, "I'm not interested."

Grandpa said, "Just because you are not interested, does not mean it won't come. Trust God."

Ben smiled and said, "Yes sir. What color car did you buy?"

Grandpa said, "Blue, you know that's Phyllis' favorite color!"

They both laughed. After work, Grandpa and Ben drove home. Mary ran out to greet him and Ben.

She hugged Ben and said, "I missed you."

Ben said, "I always miss you Mary!"

Mary smiled and said, "Grandpa, that's a nice car."

Grandpa asked, "You think your mother will like it?"

Mary exclaimed, "She's going to love it! Ben, I got my learner's permit."

Ben asked, "Can you drive yet?"

Mary said, "I'm pretty good, right Grandpa!"

Grandpa said, "She caught on quicker than you and David did!"

Ben said, "I'm not surprised. Did you cook dinner?"

Mary said, "Yes, we are having pork chops, smothered in a brown gravy, brown rice, and green beans."

Ben said, "Sounds like your cooking has improved too."

Mary laughed and said, "It had too! Now that David is gone, I have to cook Monday through Friday."

Grandpa said, "She does very good. She took all of David's healthy tips too."

When it was time to pick up Mom from the rideshare, Mary and Ben went in the new car. They stood in front of the car, so Mom would see them.

As Mom walked to meet them, she asked, "Where's the truck?"

Mary exclaimed, "Grandpa bought this new car?"

Mom said, "This is very nice and so luxurious. Dad did not tell me he was getting a new car."

Ben said, "He said he did not want you to get stranded. The other car was having some issues. He also said that he got a great deal at the Chevrolet dealership. He bought a van for the shop too."

Mom said, "Dad is always thinking of us."

Ben agreed, "I know."

Mom asked, "How are you doing Ben?"

Ben said, "I'm better. I packed up Tammy's apartment. Next weekend, I will take her things to Columbus."

Mom said, "I know that was hard. When your dad died, I could not pack up his things. Miss Bessie came down and did it for me."

Ben said, "It was hard, Caleb helped me."

Mary asked, "Did you keep anything of Tammy's for me?"

Ben said, "Yes, I did. I knew that you would want a few things."

Mary said, "Thanks Ben. It's been hard for me too, but I am getting better."

When they arrived back to the house, Grandpa was sitting on the porch.

Mom smiled and said, "Dad, you did not tell me you were buying a car."

Grandpa said, "No, I did not. I wanted it to be a surprise. Do you like it?"

Mom said, "I love it. It's blue."

Everyone said together, "That's your favorite color!"

Everyone laughed.

10

HEALING SEASON

Ben took Tammy's things to Columbus. Her family was very happy to see him. They promised to stay in contact and planned to attend his graduation in May.

Ben returned to the university feeling like he was waking up from a bad dream. He remembered everything, but was starting to feel things again. Caleb tried to keep him busy, weeks turned into months, months flew by.

David was excelling at his college in Atlanta. Everyone enjoyed the Christmas Break. It was like old times at the house. David couldn't wait to share some of his new recipes. January 1978 came quickly. Ben was on schedule to graduate in May. After two years of Spanish in conjunction with her tapes and workbooks, Mary spoke Spanish fluently. She was now a junior and taking French.

One day in January Dean Smith asked, "Ben, do you have any plans after graduation?"

Ben said, "Yes, sir. As you know my Grandpa will be eighty-six years old this year. I plan to go back to Fairville and help him at the golf shop."

Dean Smith said, "You know you could have a very lucrative career at any corporation. I have had inquiries about you already."

Ben said, "Yes sir, I know. I want to go home, run the golf shop, and spend this time with Grandpa."

Dean Smith said encouragingly, "I have several positions here at the university that I would be happy to offer you. If you don't like those, I will create one for you."

Ben smiled and said, "Thank you sir, but not right now."

Dean Smith said, "I understand your loyalty. Whenever you are ready, I would love to have you as part of my team."

Ben said, "I will keep that in mind."

Dean Smith said, "One more thing. Have you thought about getting your master's degree?"

Ben said, "I have thought about that."

Dean Smith said, "Well, I have a few scholarships, with your grades you could easily qualify for them. You can drive up and take classes two days a week."

Ben asked, "Would I have to be a full-time student to accept the scholarship or can I be part time?"

Dean Smith smiled and said, "For the last three years, Ben you have proven yourself. I would be willing to offer you a scholarship on a part time enrollment. That just means it will take you longer."

Ben said, "Let me pray about it. When do you need an answer?"

Dean Smith said, "I would need an answer by the first of July."

Ben said, "Thank you sir. I appreciate everything you have done for me."

Dean Smith smiled and said, "Ben, you are great soil to invest in. Everything you have been a part of here at the university has prospered. Investing in you brings great dividends."

Ben smiled, shook his hand, then walked away. The next few weeks went by fast.

One day Ben was at the tutoring center, a young lady walked in and said, "Hi Ben, do you remember me?"

Confused Ben looked at the young lady and said, "I am sorry, but I don't."

The young lady said, "My name is Wanda Knowlton. I used to see you at church when I was in Fairville visiting my Uncle Robert."

Ben smiled and said, "I am sorry. I remember you now. You're Mr. Knowlton's niece. The last time I saw you was the summer of 1972."

Wanda said, "You're right. That was the last time I was there. The next summer, I started working."

Ben asked, "Do you attend Middle Georgia State now?"

Wanda said, "Yes, I do. My family lives in Warner Robins. I attended a junior college there for my first two years. I started here last fall, I'm in my junior year."

Ben asked, "What is your major?"

Wanda said, "I have not made a definitive decision. On paper, I'm a business major. Truthfully, I think I want to be a teacher. I like business, but I realized that I don't want to work for a big corporation."

Ben said, "Well, you can always start your own business?"

Wanda said, "That's true. What I would really love is to have a center, where I can teach different courses. I would like to train people on the new desktop computers that are coming out now. Or help students that are struggling in certain courses. I could open an afterschool tutoring program or something like that. As you can see, I don't have a clear plan."

Ben smiled and said, "All of that sounds great."

Wanda said, "Of course my uncle told me that you attended

the university and I heard some people talking about a Ben Davis at the tutoring center. It never occurred to me that it was you. Just then when I was passing by, I saw you walk into the center."

Ben smiled and said, "It was great seeing you. I have a session in about three minutes. I hope to see you again soon.

Wanda said, "OK, do you need tutors here? I tutored at my junior college"

Ben said excitedly, "Yes, we always need tutors. Let me get Miss Tiffany to help you."

Ben told Miss Tiffany about a prospective new tutor and then went to tutor his student. Miss Tiffany reviewed Wanda's credentials and invited her to join the volunteer staff at the Tutoring Center. After Ben's tutoring session he had a break.

Miss Tiffany said, "Ben, when you first started I needed so much help. Now, I am overflowing with students and tutors. Our tutoring staff is now twenty volunteers. We tutor at least 500 students a month. I am sad this is your last year."

Ben smiled and said, "I am sure your numbers will continue to increase."

Miss Tiffany said, "That young lady, Wanda, was very impressive. She said that she knew you."

Ben said, "I used to see her during the summer when she visited Fairville. I have not seen her for six years."

Miss Tiffany said, "I'm glad, she signed up to volunteer."

One of Ben and Caleb's favorite things to do was to go to movies. They planned to see the movie 'Superman' starring Christopher Reeves.

After the movie, Caleb said, "I met a girl that I like."

Ben said, "That's great! What's her name?"

Caleb said, "Renee! She's intelligent, beautiful, funny, and classy."

Ben asked, "Where did you meet her?"

Caleb said, "We were both standing in line at the bookstore."

Ben asked, "What year is she?"

Caleb said, "She's a sophomore, majoring in Education."

Ben said, "That's great Caleb. Do you think she likes you?"

Caleb said, "Yes. She asked me if I lived on campus. Then she asked me if I wanted to have dinner with her in the cafeteria tomorrow."

Ben said, "Wow, she's a modern woman. What does she look like?"

Caleb said, "She has a small, curly afro, not the Jheri curl. You can tell she rolls her hair at night. She's about five feet, six inches tall, athletic build. She is fine!"

Ben asked, "What else do you know about her?"

Caleb said, "She has two sisters, one older and one younger."

Ben asked, "Anything else?"

Caleb laughed and said, "That's all I know now, but I will know more tomorrow night."

Ben advised, "I hope that she's the one, but don't be disappointed if she is not."

Caleb said, "I won't, but there's something special about her. I can't describe it."

Ben said, "That's what you said about Faye and what was that other girl's name? It was something French!"

Caleb said, "Oh, Chante!"

Ben said, "Yes, but both of them broke your heart."

Caleb laughed and said, "They were not right for me."

Ben asked, "What about Quitta?"

Caleb said, "Oh, she was too much for me! She had big dreams, bigger than mine. I could not keep up with her."

Ben laughed.

Caleb asked, "Have you met anyone you like yet?"

Ben said, "No, I am not interested. I'm just starting to feel normal again."

Caleb said, "I know it has been about seven months. Just don't close your heart."

Ben said, "That's similar to what Grandpa said. I don't think my heart is closed, I am just not ready yet."

More months passed, next thing you know it was time for graduation. Ben was so excited. This was his dream coming true. He always felt that he would graduate from college, but now that it was finally happening. He was so happy.

He rented a venue to celebrate his graduation. He found a caterer and decided to wear the same outfit he had worn at Tammy's graduation celebration. He made sure the room was decorated very nicely. He also hired a photographer to take pictures. He did not want Grandpa worried about taking pictures. Each morning he woke up thankful, that he was one day closer to graduating.

Finally, on the Friday night before graduation his family, Tammy's family, Caleb, other friends, Miss Tiffany, some of his instructors, and Dean Smith all gathered to celebrate his graduation. The food was delicious, everyone was having a great time.

Ben stood up and said, "I want to thank all of you for coming to help me celebrate tonight. This has been a dream that I have had for many years, and God has brought it to fruition today. All of you have supported or guided me on this journey and I just wanted to say thank you very much. I could not have gotten here without you."

Mom proudly stood up and said, "This has not only been a dream for Ben, but it has been a dream for me. Ben is the first in our family to graduate from college, but he is not the last. David will be graduating in a few years and Mary will be starting her college journey soon. This will change the future of our entire family and for that I am grateful. God has blessed above and beyond what I could have ever thought. My son, graduating Summa Cum Laude and tonight he just told me that he will start working on his master's degree in the fall. I am so happy for him."

Grandpa stood up with his handkerchief in his hand and said, "I am not surprised by anything that my oldest grandson does. He is a special young man, anointed by God to improve whatever surroundings he may find himself in. I am blessed to have him in my life. I asked God to let me live long enough to see him graduate from college and God has answered my prayer. I am so proud of him."

Dean Smith stood up and said, "I met Ben on his second day of class here at the university. I found him to be impressive, intelligent, considerate, and dedicated. I have now known him for three years and I am even more impressed with him. I was not ready to let him go. I offered him a job, I told him that I would create a job for him!"

Everyone laughed.

Dean Smith continued, "However, then my last option was to offer him a scholarship to get his master's degree. I was afraid he was going to say no to that too. When he asked if he could go to school part time. I immediately said yes. I just wanted him to be a part of this university a little longer. Mr. Cason is correct, he improves whatever situation he finds himself in. Our university is better because of him."

Miss Tiffany stood up and said, "Dean Smith is right, I was struggling at the Tutoring Center before Ben started volunteering there. I almost let him go when he said that he was a freshman. Usually we don't allow freshmen to tutor other students. Something deep inside told me to allow him to take the test. I am so glad that I did. He quickly established a reputation of the best tutor we have ever had. Over the last three years, we have tutored more students than the seven years before combined. It all started when Ben joined our team. We are going to miss you Ben. However, we know that success follows you. Just drop by whenever you can to say hello."

Ben smiled.

Ben stood up and said, "You have all said such wonderful things about me. I appreciate you taking the time to get to know me. As I stated before, my plan is to return home to Fairville to help my Grandpa with his Golf Shop and I will be working on my Master's degree part time. I would love to have a picture of all of us. Please join me over on that wall for a photo."

After the photograph was taken, everyone mingled and talked until it was ten o'clock. Everyone helped with the cleanup of the room before they left. Ben had reserved hotel rooms for his family, so they would not have to drive back to Fairville.

The graduation was long, there were 1,100 graduates. Ben graduated with every honor possible. After graduation, so many people wanted to shake his hand and congratulate him. Everyone was so proud of him. He was also proud of himself.

After the graduation everyone headed home. There was a convoy of Ben and Mary in his truck, David in his truck, and Mom drove Grandpa in the car.

David stayed home only for the weekend, he still had two more weeks of class before the summer break. Ben settled into his room that was shared with Grandpa. Mary was still in school for two more weeks but she was excited about her summer camp.

She was now sixteen and Mom had approved a two-week

summer camp in Athens, Georgia. This camp focused on the new desktop computers that were becoming popular. Mary would learn how to use the computer and teach others. Mary also found a job for the summer. She and Becky would be working with Mr. Knowlton again, but this time they would be updating the high school library.

Mr. Hank Jennings had more paperwork for Ben to sign, Grandpa was very happy that Ben was home.

11

CHANGES

One night during the first week of July 1978, David was serving dinner. Everyone was so happy that Ben was home! At the dinner table, Mary said, "Grandpa, tell us another story about your family."

Grandpa said, "Well, I have told you so many already. I have not told you about when my father first came to America. It was in 1892. My father and his brother with their wives came to America on a ship, through Ellis Island. They had traveled many months to get here from Scotland."

Mary said, "I may try to go to Scotland one day."

Everyone laughed.

Grandpa continued, "They could not carry much since they were traveling so far, but they were able to bring a few family heirlooms."

David asked, "What type of heirlooms? Do you still have them?"

Grandpa said, "They brought candlesticks, some vases, jewelry, and a few small statues. Some of them were very valuable. They settled in New York City. My mother did not like it there, it was too crowded. My uncle and his wife did not want to leave. My father and mother headed south. They traveled on the train until they got to Atlanta. It was not an easy trip, but my mother did not want to live in cold weather. When they arrived in Atlanta, my mother was eight months pregnant. My father knew he had to find a place to call home soon. He met a man that had a horse and wagon and was on his way to Fairville. My dad asked him a few questions. He then decided that Fairville was the place for him and my mother. They caught a ride with that man, he was black. He was very nice to my parents. When they arrived in Fairville, that man gave my parents shelter until I was born. My dad worked in the fields until he could do better. That man helped my dad find a place to live and get him settled. My parents raised me to believe that all people are created equal. It was a culture shock for my parents to find so much prejudice in the south. However, they liked Fairville and were determined to make a home here. In 1901 my dad opened the golf shop and when he died, he passed it on to me.

Mary said, "I like that story."

Ben asked, "Do you know the black man's name that helped your dad?"

Grandpa said, "Yes, his name was John Thomas Baldwin. He had a brother named Jeremiah. My dad said that John T. died in 1905."

Mom asked, "Do you know how he died?"

Grandpa said, "Yes, he was lynched by the Klu Klux Klan. My dad helped him start a blacksmith business."

Mary said, "That is so sad."

Mom said, "It is sad. So many of our ancestors were killed because of prejudice. I am so thankful that things have changed."

Grandpa said, "Me too!"

Mary said, "Grandpa, I love you!"

David went over to Grandpa and gave him a big hug then said, "I love you too!"

Everyone showered Grandpa with hugs and kisses.

Grandpa pulled his handkerchief out of his pocket and said, "I love you all more than you can ever imagine."

On the next morning, it was obvious that Grandpa was not doing well. He tried his best to hide it. Ben took him to the doctor. Dr. Little said that his heart and kidneys were shutting down, this was common in diabetes patients.

Grandpa knew that his days were numbered. He had no regrets, he had asked God to allow him to see Ben graduate from college and he did. When Grandpa was at the shop, Ben saw him constantly writing something. Ben did not ask, but felt that it was out of the ordinary for him to spend so much time writing. Ben worked hard to make sure everything was taken care of.

One day Grandpa asked, "Ben, do you have any ideas about expanding the golf shop."

Ben replied, "In one of my business classes, we were talking about when is a good time to expand a business or start a new business. My instructor said that if your profit margin was continually rising each year, it was safe to expand."

Grandpa said, "Well, our profit margin has increased every year for the last six years."

Ben said, "The instructor also said that it would take capital to get the expansion or second business going, so you have to determine if you have enough. Or if you need to secure a loan."

Grandpa said, "That is true. Let's suppose you have the capital and the location, what would you like to do?"

Ben said, "I was thinking that we could expand into other

sports. There is a vacant building next door. It's much bigger than the golf shop. We could make that location into other sporting goods like basketball, soccer, or baseball equipment. If we don't have it on hand, we could order it."

Grandpa said, "That's a great idea. I know that I won't live long enough to see you do that, so I already bought the location next door. I want you to create a plan of what you will need, the cost, the renovation, and everything else to create that sporting goods store."

Surprised Ben asked, "Grandpa, when did you buy the building?"

Grandpa said, "When you first went off to college. The previous owner gave me a great deal, so I bought it."

Ben said excitedly, "Grandpa, you are always thinking. I want to be just like you?"

Grandpa said, "Son, you are more than on your way of exceeding all that I have done. I am very proud of you."

Ben said, "I will start researching and creating a business plan."

Grandpa said, "Remember, if you ever need any help just talk to Hank Jennings. I trust him. Also, do you remember, Timothy Stevens, my accountant. His office is on Highway 15."

Ben said, "Yes sir. I remember."

Grandpa said, "Those are the two men that I trust. You can trust them too."

Ben said, "Yes sir. Grandpa, I know that your health is failing. I'm trying to prepare myself, but I also have to be realistic. Is there anything special you want for your funeral?"

Grandpa said, "Ben, I have been thinking about that too. I don't want a lot of fuss. I created a list of people I do want you to notify. If they can attend the funeral fine, if not that is fine too. I would like a graveside funeral, simple but tasteful. I already have a plot next to my wife at the Holy Cross Cemetery. I have also paid for the services to prepare the body at Hicks Funeral Home and I already picked out my casket."

Ben asked, "When did you do all of this?"

Grandpa said, "I did it a long time ago, when my wife died. I checked last month to make sure that they still had my account and that everything was still valid."

Ben said, 'Wow!"

Grandpa said, "I already paid for the flowers that I want too. I checked with the florist. My account is still valid, so all you have to do is notify these people."

Ben said, "Grandpa, part of me is glad that you have done all of this. Of course, I would have gotten it done, but it would be very hard. I don't want you to die."

Grandpa said, "I know son. Dying is part of living. God has blessed me with a good life. He even gave me a daughter and three grandchildren, that I thought I would never have. Since I have been living with you all, I have renewed my relationship with Christ. I am ready to go. I know it's time. Our bodies can't last forever, but mine has lasted for eighty-six years."

Ben wiped the tears from his face and said, "I knew that I had to finish college early."

Grandpa said, "Always listen to your intuition, that's God leading you. Don't listen to other people when it's something that you feel strongly about."

Ben said, "I am glad that I didn't."

Grandpa said, "I have written letters to Phyllis, David, Mary, and you. I don't want you to open them until then. I have also written down all of the contacts for the florist, funeral home, and cemetery plot."

Ben said, "Yes sir."

Grandpa said, "You know I have turned all that I have over

to you. Hank will advise you and break down exactly what is involved. My house is paid for. You may not want to live in my neighborhood, some of my neighbors are really prejudice. I barely wanted to live next to them."

Ben laughed.

Grandpa continued, "You can sell the house and take the money to buy you another one if you like. It is up to you. You can also rent the house if you like."

Ben smiled.

Grandpa said, "Ben, as knowledgeable as you are, you are still very young. I want you to talk to your mother about major decisions. She is very wise."

Ben said, "Yes sir. I will."

Grandpa said, "Dr. Little told me that death could come at any time. I could not wake up in the morning or I could be wide awake when it happens."

Ben said, "I don't want you to be in any pain."

Grandpa said, "I'm very tired and I do experience some discomfort but overall I am fine."

Ben said, "Grandpa, you know how much I love you and how thankful I am for all that you have done for me."

Grandpa said, "I know. You also know how much I love you, and how thankful I am to you for all that you have done for me."

Ben said, "I know."

Grandpa said, "Then, I can relax that you know. Again, I have no regrets."

Ben said, "Grandpa, you know that I will work hard to keep your business thriving."

Grandpa said, "I know. I also know that God's hand is on you and you will take all that I have to the next level."

Ben said, "I have to go to the bank to make a deposit."

Grandpa said, "No problem. David made us lunch, we can eat when you get back."

Ben hugged his grandpa tightly and said, "That sounds great. I will be right back."

When Ben returned, Grandpa was sitting at the counter. He noticed that he was quiet. When he got closer, he saw that he had died. Ben dropped to the floor and cried. He was inconsolable. He thought he had prepared himself for this. He realized that you can never be prepared for death. When he was able to stop crying, he picked up the phone and dialed 911. The paramedics pronounced Grandpa dead and took him to the hospital. Ben contacted Hicks funeral home to let them know. It was five o'clock, he closed up the shop and headed home to give his family the news.

Mary and David ran out to meet his truck. They could tell something was wrong, when they did not see Grandpa on the passenger side.

Mary asked, "Where's Grandpa?"

David asked, "Did something happen?"

Ben said sadly, "Yes, Grandpa passed away at the shop this afternoon."

Mary screamed and ran in the house to her room and cried.

David asked, "Ben, how did it happen?"

Ben said, "It was a normal day, we talked about a lot of things. He told me the things he wanted for his funeral. Then I left to go make a bank deposit, and when I got back. He had died sitting at the counter."

David said, "I knew it was coming soon. I could see how he had slowed down. Did he seem in pain?"

Ben said, "I asked him the same thing, he said he was very tired and had a little discomfort, but no major pain."

David said, "I'm glad."

Ben hugged his brother and they both cried. Since Ben's graduation, Mom had been driving the car to work. Grandpa would ride with Ben to work. When the car pulled up in front of the house, Ben ran out to greet his mother. David and Mary were still trying to process the news.

Ben said sadly, "Hi Mom."

Mom said, "Hey baby! Where's everybody?"

Ben said, "Mary is in the bathroom and David is in the kitchen."

It was not like her children to not greet her, Mom asked, "What's wrong?"

Ben suggested, "Come on into the house."

Mom demanded, "No, tell me what is wrong!"

Ben said, "Grandpa died this afternoon."

Mom stumbled, Ben caught her. As he held her up, she felt her body go limp. He helped her up the steps. They sat on the porch.

Mom said, "I knew it was getting close."

Ben said, "We all did. We were just talking today in the shop. He told me what he wanted for his funeral and some other things. I went to the bank. When I returned, he had died. He was sitting at the counter."

Mom said, "Ben, he knew how much we loved him."

Ben said, "Yes ma'am he did. He also knew that we knew how much he loved us."

Mom said, "My heart is breaking again. We were just getting over Tammy's death. God! Help us!"

Ben said, "I know. Mary is still crying in her room and David is in the kitchen crying."

Mom said, "I know death is part of life, but that does not make it any easier."

Ben said, "No ma'am it doesn't. I thought I had prepared

myself, but when I found him at the shop, I realized that we are never prepared."

Mom said, "That's true. Did you call 911 and notify the funeral home."

Ben said, "Yes ma'am I did. He's now at the morgue at the hospital waiting for Hicks Funeral Home to pick him up."

Mom said, "Today is Monday, I will take off the rest of the week from work, so we can make the arrangements."

Ben said, "Yes ma'am. He gave me a list of people he wanted me to notify. I will call them tomorrow."

Mom stood up and said, "I can go in the house now."

As they entered the house, David ran to greet his mother.

Crying David said, "Mom, this is very hard."

Mom hugged him and said, "Yes, it is, but God will get us through it."

Mary heard her mother's voice and ran in the room, wiping her tears, she said, "Mom, I can't take any more death."

Mom agreed, "I know. Hopefully, we won't have to take any more for a very long time."

David said, "We don't have to have dinner if you don't want too."

Mom said, "I think we should. We can talk about Dad and the things we need to do at the table."

David said, "I made chicken and dumplings with English peas for dinner."

Ben said, "It smells delicious. I did not get a chance to eat lunch. So, I am a little hungry."

Mom said, "Let me wash up and I will meet you all at the table."

Everyone was seated at the table; Grandpa's chair was empty.

Mom said, "I think we need to start today with a prayer, everyone please hold hands. Lord, we thank you for the life of

Charlie Cason. We thank you for allowing us to get to know him and love him for the last six years. God, we ask you for strength to go through this difficult time. Help us to reflect on the fact that now Dad is with you and he is in no more pain. God mend our hearts, for right now they are broken. Help us to perform the tasks we need to do for the funeral. We trust you Father, In Jesus Name we pray. Amen."

Everyone said, "Amen."

Mom said, "It is OK for us to feel sad, we loved Dad. It is important to remember that death is a part of life and as difficult as it is, we have to understand that our lives do not stop now. God has plans for each of us. Do whatever you need to do to grieve, but don't stop living. Dad would not want that for any of us."

Ben said, "Thank you mom, that helps. Grandpa gave me letters for each of us."

Mom said, "That was so sweet of him to take the time to write each of us a letter. Let's read the letters after dinner. David has prepared a delicious meal for us."

Mary said, "I'm just as sad now as I was when Tammy died."

Mom said, "That's because you loved both Tammy and Dad. Now when you are not as close to someone when they pass, it's different."

David said, "When I was at the Institute, a student down the hall choked and died. I was sad that he died, but I did not know him. So, I did not feel the feeling I'm feeling now."

Mom said, "That's right. The important thing is that when a person dies, we want them to have given their life to Christ so they can go to heaven."

Ben said, "Grandpa said he did that. He said that he renewed his relationship with Christ after he moved in with us."

Mom said, "I know. We talked about it one night. So, we can find joy in knowing that we will see Grandpa again, when we get to heaven."

Mary said, "Well, I don't want any of you to go any time soon."

Everyone laughed.

After dinner, everyone gathered in the living room. Ben passed out each letter.

Mom suggested, "Let's read each of our letters silently. If you want to share what Dad said, you can."

Everyone read their letters and cried.

Mom said, "Dad, told me how much he loved me and that I was the best daughter he could have asked for. He also paid off the house. He said, that now that he was not here to pay the increased utility bills, that he did not want me to pay the bills and a house note. He also deposited some money in my bank account to cover anything that I may ever need or want. The car was already in my name."

Ben said, "That was so sweet Mom! Grandpa was always thinking about us."

Wiping her eyes, Mom said, "Yes he was. God has blessed us through him"

David said, "In my letter, he told me how proud of me he was. He also said that my cooking had prolonged his life and for me to continue cooking healthy. He said that he knew that I wanted to open a place of my own, that he had purchased the old City Café. After I completed culinary school, that if I wanted to, I could open a bakery or café of my own. He said that he had created a trust that would be available to me when I graduated from culinary school. That would be enough money to renovate the place. He also said, that if I did not want to open my own place in Fairville, that I could sell the building back to Ben. Whatever I decided would be fine with him. He told me that he loved me very much."

Mom said, "He bought you a building. Wow! That is awesome David."

David said, "I know. I do want to open a place here in Fairville. I want to serve soup, sandwiches, and desserts."

Mary said, "That's a great idea."

Mom said, "You could also sell your cakes too!"

David said excitedly, "I know. When I get back to the Institute, I will start working on a business plan."

Mary said, "My letter told me how much he loved me and how proud of me he was too. He said that his vocabulary had increased since he met me."

Everyone laughed.

Mary continued, "He also said, that he had created a trust for me too, that would be available to me when I graduated from college. However, a special account had been set up for me to purchase a car when I graduate from high school. That would be his graduation gift to me. He said that he knows that I will be successful in all that I do. That for me to consider majoring in linguistics at college. He could see me being an interpreter for the government. He also said that he is so proud to call me his granddaughter."

Surprised Mom said, "Wow, he set up a trust for you too. That is wonderful. I guess since he gave the boys a vehicle for their graduation gift, he could not leave you out."

Ben said, "In my letter he tells me how much he loved me. He said that me coming to work for him in 1972 changed his life. That he realized it was a gift from God. He is so thankful. He has enjoyed watching me grow up into the man that God has called me to be. He is so thankful that I showed him love in spite of his skin color. He said that he trusts that I will always be there for the family and that any decisions that I make concerning all that he has turned over to me will be fine with him. That he trusts me. He also told me to keep my heart open. That God has a woman for me that will make me happier than I ever thought I would be. He said that I have sown too many seeds of love for God not to bless me."

Mom said, "He is right. When you were looking for a job, I told you to work hard and show your boss that he could depend on you and prove that you were the best employee he had ever had. You did that! Because of your dedication, God has blessed you and our family."

Ben said, "Mom, this is so much to digest."

Mom said, "God's hand is on you. He has prepared you even though you may think you can't handle it. You have people to guide you, so you are not alone. Don't worry, God will continue to lead you."

Mom stood up and everyone hugged each other.

David said, "I did not know that Grandpa had this much money."

Mom said, "None of us did, we loved him because of who he was, not because of what he had."

12

PREPARING FOR THE FUNERAL

Early the next day, Ben and his mom went to the funeral home to discuss the funeral arrangements.

Charlie Hicks said "Hello Ms. Davis and Ben. I am so sorry that I have to see you under these circumstances."

Mom said, "Good Morning!"

Ben said, "Mr. Hicks have you been able to go get the body yet."

Charlie Hicks said, "Yes, it was released to us last night. Would you like to see him?"

Mom said, "Not right now. I plan to go shopping today to purchase a suit for Dad to wear. Is there anything particular that I need to know?"

As he passed Mom a piece of paper, Charlie Hicks said, "Yes, this will tell you everything you need to know."

Mom said, "Thank you."

Charlie Hicks asked, "When would you like to have the ceremony?"

Ben asked, "What dates do you have available?"

Charlies Hicks said, "We can do Saturday at one o'clock.

That would give us more than enough time. We can have Mr. Cason ready for viewing early on Friday."

Mom said, "That would be fine."

Charlie Hicks said, "We will print a program for you. All I need is a picture and his biography information."

Ben passed Mr. Hicks a picture and a piece of paper and said, "Here you are."

Charlie Hicks said, "OK, Phyllis if you can stop by later today with the clothing, I will take care of everything else."

Ben said, "I know Grandpa paid for all of his services. I would like to add that throw I saw in the lobby."

Charlie Hicks said, "That would be a beautiful keepsake. Unfortunately, we have to order it, so it will not be back by the weekend. I will place the order. Would you like for us to use this same picture on the throw?"

Ben said, "Yes, that will be fine."

Mom stood up and said, "I will be back later today. Oh, do I need to contact the florist or will you?"

Charlie Hicks said, "I will take care of all of that. I will see you later today."

Mom and Ben left the funeral home. They returned home to tell the family about the arrangements. As they drove up, David and Mary ran out of the house.

David hugged his mother and asked, "Did you have any problems?"

Mom said, "No, there was not much to do. Dad had taken care of picking out the casket he wanted. We just needed to agree on a date."

Mary asked, "Did you pick this Saturday?"

Mom said, "Yes, we did. How did you know?"

Mary said, "Most people don't wait a long time before they bury someone."

Mom said, "That's correct. You only wait a long time if you are waiting for someone to come from out of town."

As they walked in the house, Mom said, "Oh, I just thought of something?"

Ben asked, "Did we leave something at the funeral home?"

Mom said, "No, we need a place to have a repass after the funeral."

Ben said, "Oh, I really don't know how many people will come to the funeral."

Mom said, "I'm sure there will be many. Dad has had his golf shop for at least fifty years. He knows a lot of people in town."

Ben said, "We don't have a place here in Fairville that we can rent. The golf shop is too small."

Mom said, "You said that you were going to tell Hank Jennings about the funeral. Ask him! Maybe he knows about something we don't."

Ben said, "Yes, ma'am."

David said, "Even if we find a place, we still need a caterer."

Mary asked, "Can you cook the food?"

David said, "I guess I could do it. Today is Tuesday, that gives me three days to prepare everything. I would need some help."

Mary exclaimed, "I can help!"

Mom said, "David, that is taking on a lot. Are you sure that you can do it?"

David said, "If I make the menu simple, I can."

Ben suggested, "OK, what about your spaghetti and meatballs with a salad and some dinner rolls?"

Mom said, "That would be fine. Most people like spaghetti. Would you be able to make some cakes for dessert?"

David said, "Yes, I can do that. I may be able to make some

simple side dishes too, like corn on the cob or some green beans."

Mary suggested, "We need to go shopping!"

David said, "Yes, we do. Mom, how many do I cook for?"

Mom said, "I really don't know. Let's prepare for at least seventy-five. Do you need money to buy supplies?"

David said, "No ma'am, I still have money from the monthly food budget and I also have money in my account."

Mom said, "Whatever you spend, I will reimburse you later."

Ben said, "I need to go find a place for the repass and call the people on Grandpa's list to give them details about the funeral."

Mom said, "Don't forget to call Tammy's parents."

Ben said, "I won't. They probably won't be able to come, but I will let them know."

Everyone left to take care of their responsibilities.

It was now after ten o'clock in the morning, Ben walked into the courthouse. Mr. Jennings was standing in the hallway.

Mr. Jennings said, "Ben, I heard about Mr. Cason, I am so sorry for your loss."

Ben said, "Thank you, I came by to let you know when the ceremony would be."

Mr. Jennings said, "Please step into my office."

Mr. Jennings pointed to a seat.

Ben sat down and said, "Grandpa wanted a graveside ceremony; it will be on Saturday at one o'clock at the Holy Cross Cemetery."

Mr. Jennings said, "Thank you for letting me know. I will be there. If you don't mind, I will also share this info with others. There are many people in Fairville that would like to pay their respects. Charlie Cason was a wonderful man."

Ben said, "Yes sir, he was."

Mr. Jennings asked, "How are you and your family doing?"

Ben said, "As well as can be expected. I think I am all cried out."

Mr. Jennings asked, "Do you need any help with anything?"

Ben said, "The funeral is under control. I need a place to hold the repass. I don't know of any place in Fairville, that is big enough to hold about seventy-five people. I thought about the fellowship hall at my church, but I'm sure some of the Fairville citizens will not want to come to my church."

Mr. Jennings laughed and said, "You are probably right. I do know a place. I think you should plan for more like one hundred and fifty people. I have a client that just built a place designed for large parties or events. He has not rented it to anyone yet, but I do feel that he will rent it to you."

Ben asked, "Is it here in Fairville?"

Mr. Jennings said, "Yes, it is. On Highway 15, have you noticed the new building on the right? The address is 3232 Highway 15."

Ben said, "Yes, I saw it, but I did not know what it was. There was no sign out front."

Mr. Jennings said, "You are right, but the inside is finished."

Ben asked, "Do I need to get tables and chairs?"

Mr. Jennings said, "No, it has everything you will need already. There are two event rooms and two kitchens?"

Ben said, "Two kitchens! Wow! Here in Fairville! Will they lease to blacks?"

Mr. Jennings smiled and said, "Yes, they will."

Ben asked, "Who do I contact?"

Mr. Jennings said, "Let me make a call. When do you need the place?"

Ben said, "I would like to see it today. My brother, David,

is catering. He had planned to cook at the house. If it has a kitchen, maybe he could cook there?"

Mr. Jennings asked, "How about I get the keys for you today. Can you stop back by in about an hour or so?"

Ben said, "Yes sir. I don't want to get too excited. Are you sure this is a possibility?"

Mr. Jennings said, "Yes, don't worry about a thing. All I ask is that after you have finished, clean the place up by Tuesday of next week."

Ben said, "That will be great. Mr. Jennings, it does not matter the cost. We need a nice place for Grandpa, so I am willing to pay whatever the fee is."

Mr. Jennings said, "The fee is reasonable, but we will take care of that later. Also, next week, can you come by for me to fill you in on everything?"

Ben said, "Yes, sir! I can."

Mr. Jennings looked at this calendar and asked, "How about ten o'clock Tuesday morning?"

Ben stood up and said, "That would be fine."

He shook Mr. Jennings hand and said, "I will see you in an hour or so."

Mr. Jennings said, "I look forward to it?"

Ben left the office excited that he had a place for the repass. As he was walking to the car, he saw Wanda Knowlton.

Ben said, "Hello Wanda!"

Wanda turned around and said, "Hi Ben. You remember my cousin, Dee."

Ben said, "Of course I do. Hi Dee!"

Dee said, "Hi Ben."

Wanda said, "Ben, I just heard about your Grandpa, I am so sorry for your loss."

Ben said, "Thanks! What are you doing in Fairville?"

Wanda said, "I had a job for the summer at home in Warner Robins. The main water pipe burst at the building where I worked. All of the damage is diluvial. The repairs will take about three weeks, maybe a month. I decided to come visit my Uncle Robert. I have been here for about three days."

Ben said, "It's good to see you again."

Wanda asked, "Do you need any help with anything for your Grandpa?"

Ben said, "No, we have the funeral under control. I just secured a place to hold the repass. David will be catering."

Dee said, "David! I didn't see him at church on Sunday, I thought he had gone back to Atlanta."

Ben said, "No, he has about five more weeks before school starts."

Wanda said, "When my grandmother died last year, we had everything covered except one thing. We had a hard time trying to find someone to set up the food for the repass. Everyone wanted to attend the funeral."

Ben said, "I had not thought about that."

Wanda said, "I will set up the food for you. Dee, will you help me?"

Dee said, "Yes, I will help. My friend Pam will be happy to help too."

Ben said, "I can't ask you to do that?"

Wanda said, "You're not asking, we're volunteering. We did not know your Grandpa that well, so we're willing to miss the funeral."

Ben said, "I really do appreciate it Wanda!"

Wanda said, "No problem at all. Where will the repass be?"

Ben said, "There is a new building on Highway 15, the address is 3232."

Dee said, "I know where that is. There is no sign out front."

Ben laughed and said, "I know. It's not opened yet. They are willing to lease it to me. I will pick up the key in about an hour."

Wanda said, "That's great. Are you going there today?"

Ben said, "Yes, I will go tell my family and I hope that we can go there around one o'clock."

Wanda asked, "Can we meet you there?"

Ben said, "You don't have to."

Dee asked, "Will David be there too?"

Ben smiled and said, "Yes!"

Wanda said, "As you can see, Dee has a crush on your brother!"

Ben laughed and said, "I can see!"

Wanda said, "We did not have anything planned today. Then we can see if David needs help with anything else."

Ben reached over and hugged Wanda, he said, "Thank you so much!"

Wanda said, "I'm glad that we can help. See you around one o'clock."

Ben walked to his truck and drove away.

When he arrived home, Mom was already there. Ben walked into the house to find his family busy.

Mom asked, "Did you find a place?"

Ben said, "Yes, I did. Mr. Jennings was a great help. There is a new place on Highway 15."

Mom said, "I saw that place. It doesn't have a sign out front."

Ben laughed and said, "I know. I can pick up the key in about thirty minutes. Can everyone go to look at it around one o'clock?"

David said, "That will be fine."

Mom said, "I'm free too."

Ben said, "I ran into Wanda Knowlton in town. She and her cousin, Dee, volunteered to set up the repass for us while we are at the funeral."

Mom said, "I can't believe that I did not think of that."

Ben said, "I didn't either. They will also get Dee's friend, Pam, to help. They will meet us there at one o'clock."

Mom said, "That's great!"

Ben said, "David, you know Dee has a crush on you."

David said, "That girl has had a crush on me since I was in the ninth grade and she was in the fifth."

Ben said, "I just wanted to warn you."

Everyone laughed.

Ben said, "Mr. Jennings said that we should prepare for 150 people."

David exclaimed "One hundred and fifty people! Wow! Mary and I will have to go back to the store."

Ben said, "This place also has a kitchen. Maybe you can cook the food there!"

David said, "A kitchen, wow! I can't wait to see this place."

Ben went back to town to pick up the key to the building. He stopped by the golf shop and called all of the people on Grandpa's list. They all said that they would see him on Saturday. Tammy's parents said they would not be able to come, but they wanted to send a flower arrangement. Ben met his family at the building at one o'clock. They were waiting in the parking lot when he arrived. Shortly after, Wanda, Dee and Pam drove up. Everyone greeted each other in the parking lot.

Mom said, "Wanda, it's good to see you again. It's been a long time."

Wanda hugged Mom and said, "It has been a long time. It seems like you are getting younger each year."

Mom smiled and said, "The Holy Spirit is a preserver!"

Everyone laughed.

Mom said, "Wanda, you have developed into a beautiful young woman."

Wanda said, "Thank you. Uncle Robert said that I look like my grandmother."

Dee said, "Hi David!"

David said, "Hi Dee. Thanks for helping us out."

Dee said, "No problem. Everyone, this is Pam, my best friend."

Mary said, "I know Pam. I tutored you in Latin last year."

Pam said, "I know. Thanks for your help, I got an A in the class."

Mom asked, "Dee, what grade are you in now?"

Dee said, "Pam and I are both sophomores."

Mom said, "Great. Is everyone ready to go inside and look at this new building?"

Ben unlocked the door and found the light switch. Everyone oohed and awed.

Mom said, "This is the nicest event building I have ever seen. Not that I have seen many, but this is very nice."

There was a large foyer and two different hallways. Each hallway lead to a different room. One of the rooms could accommodate groups of less than one hundred. The other room could accommodate groups of 100–300 people.

As they all walked through the space, they continued to ooh and awe.

Finally, Ben said, "This looks like the biggest room. It may be too big for what we need."

Mom said, "Mr. Jennings said to prepare for 150 people, if we use this big room, it won't be crowded. David what do you think?"

David said, "Mom, I am in awe."

Mary proclaimed, "I think we should use the big room. I think there will be about 200 people on Saturday."

Ben said, "I agree with Mary. Everyone I called said they would be here. It's better to be prepared."

Wanda said, "When we had the repass for my grandmother last year, we had more people attend than we expected."

Mom said, "That settles it, we will use the big room."

Ben exclaimed, "Wow, the tables are already set up."

Mary said, "This closet has table cloths in it. There are also plates, glasses, and cutlery. There are even cloth napkins."

David said, "We have an event room at the culinary school. It is nothing like this. This is very nice."

Mom said, "Let's check out the kitchen."

Ben opened the door to the kitchen, everything was so shiny and new. There were three very large commercial refrigerators. There were two stoves, each had six eyes. There was an industrial dishwasher and four prep tables.

David said, "These refrigerators are called coolers. Usually there is a freezer somewhere."

Mary said, "I found it. It's a walk-in freezer."

Mom asked, "Ben, are you sure we can afford this?"

Ben said, "Mr. Jennings said that the cost would be reasonable. All he asked is that we clean up by Tuesday of next week."

Mom said, "Everyone please come here."

Everyone walked closer to Mom.

Mom said, "Please hold hands so we can pray. God, thank you for providing such a nice space for us to have the repass for Dad. This is above and beyond what we could have asked for. We ask that you help us prepare enough food for the guests so that we can celebrate the life of Charlie Cason. In Jesus name we pray, Amen."

Everyone said, "Amen!"

Wanda said, "I have a great idea. Pam, Dee, and I should dress in white shirts and black pants."

David said, "That would give a really professional look. If we are going to prepare for 200 people, I think we will need a little more help, maybe two more people."

Pam said, "I'm sure my sisters will help. They are twelve and thirteen years old."

Mom said, "This is a lot of responsibility for someone so young."

Mary said, "I am sure Becky and her mother, Miss Tammy, will help."

Mom said, "Great idea, I will ask them tonight. However, to be on the safe side, maybe we should still use Pam's sisters. We can assign them some easy tasks."

Ben asked, "David, do you want to cook here or at home?"

David said, "It would be easier to cook here, then we would not have to transport the food."

Mom said, "I think so too."

Wanda suggested, "We can help you cook on Friday if you like."

David said, "I think I may need you. Even though it's a simple menu, it would make it easier on me if I had help."

Wanda said, "No problem! What time do you want us here on Friday?"

David asked, "Is nine o'clock too early for you? It will take us about six hours."

Dee smiled and said, "We will be here."

David said, "Tomorrow is Wednesday, Mary and I will go shopping. That gives us Thursday to prep all of the ingredients and bake some cakes. Then we can actually start cooking the food on Friday morning."

Dee said, "I can help you all week."

David said, "That's OK, if you all can be here on Friday, that would be great."

Mom asked, "What time do you need them here on Saturday? The ceremony is at one o'clock. We should be back here by two o'clock."

David said, "We should be finished cooking everything on Friday, so all they will have to do is warm up the sauce and meatballs. If they could set up the buffet tables with the salad, bread, and cake then turn the stove on to start boiling the water about one thirty, I will cook the noodles when I get here. So, if they are here by twelve noon. They can have everything ready by two o'clock."

Mom said, "We have a plan. Anyone has any questions or suggestions?"

Mary said, "In one of the books I read last year, they had a funeral for this famous man. They put pictures on a table for the guests to see."

Ben said, "That's a great idea Mary. We have a lot of pictures we can put on a table."

Mom said, "I think it would be better if the pictures were in frames instead of photo albums. I will take about ten of the pictures that show Dad's life and put them in frames."

Mary said, "Some are already in frames."

Mom said, "I know. Let's put a table in the foyer, so people can see the pictures when they walk in."

Ben said, "We need to have some type of agenda for the repass."

Wanda said, "For my grandmother's repass, people came in at different times. After most of the people had eaten, my Dad stood up and said thank you to all the people for coming and asked if anyone wanted to say something."

Mom said, "That sounds great. We will greet the people as they come in. Even if all of the people have not arrived, we can have Reverend King say grace over the food. Then people can go through the buffet line where you ladies will serve them. Later Ben, you can say a few words and ask if anyone wants to say anything."

Ben said, "That will be fine."

Mary asked, "What will we serve to drink?"

David asked, "How about sweet tea and water?"

Mom said, "Simple. I like it."

Wanda said, "This is a big place. You may need some type of microphone."

Ben said, "You're right. Do you think this place has one already?"

Mary exclaimed, "It has everything else."

Everyone looked around the room, finally Dee said, "I found something in this closet."

Ben rushed over and said, "Yes, that's a podium with a microphone that you plug in."

Mom said, "Whoever owns this building has thought of everything."

Ben said, "I know."

David said, "I even saw an ice machine in the kitchen. It's already plugged in and producing ice. I also saw a washer and dryer to wash the table cloths."

Mom asked, "Does anyone have any other suggestions or questions?"

No one said a thing.

Mom said, "Well, we have our assignments. Ladies, I can't thank you enough for your help. Make sure you wear comfortable shoes on Saturday."

Everyone hugged each other. Dee could not wait to hug David. David quickly pulled away.

Ben walked Wanda to her car and opened her car door, then he said, "Wanda, I can't tell you how much your help means to me. Thank you again."

Wanda said, "I'm just glad that I was here to help. Will you be here on Friday to help cook?"

Ben said, "Yes, this is the first big event that David has done. I want to help him as much as I can."

Wanda said, "Great, see you then!"

The next few days went by fast. Mary and David shopped for supplies. Mom prepared the pictures. Ben worked at the golf shop on Wednesday and Thursday. He knew customers would be coming by. He told people the news. He also called Mr. Hicks to tell him to expect more people for the funeral. Mr. Hicks said that he could put out one hundred chairs for the ceremony, but that was all he could do. That he would print about 200 programs.

Early Friday morning the family went to the funeral home to review the body. It was very emotional. Mr. Hicks did a great job preparing the body. Grandpa looked very handsome. His hair and beard were trimmed very neatly. He looked winsome in his blue suit.

Everyone cried and spent private time with Grandpa. After the viewing, it was time to go to the event center to start cooking. David and Mary had cooked the cakes on Thursday. When they drove up to the building, Wanda, Pam, and Dee were already in the parking lot.

Everyone greeted each other.

Wanda could tell that everyone had been crying, she asked, "Are you all just coming from the funeral home?"

Mom said, "Yes, Mr. Hicks did a great job on Dad."

Mary said, "I was doing fine until I saw him today."

David said, "Me too"

Wanda said, "I know it is hard. I thought I was finished crying until I saw my grandmother that Friday before the funeral."

Mom said, "I'm glad that we have work to do, that will take our minds off of it for a while."

David asked encouragingly, "Is everyone ready to get to work?"

Everyone laughed and said loudly, "Yes, chef!"

David laughed and said, "That sounds good!"

Everyone entered the building. David gave out assignments and everyone proceeded to work.

Wanda and Ben were assigned to prepare the buffet tables with chafing dishes, plates, cutlery, napkins, and glasses.

While they worked Wanda and Ben talked about different things. They prepared a beverage table separate from the food tables. They put table cloths on all of the tables. Each table seated ten people. They also found centerpieces in another closet. Twenty tables were prepared. There were five more tables in the room. They moved the five tables to another room. They also placed a six-foot table in the foyer for the pictures. Mr. Hicks had given Ben a guest book that he could use for people to sign in. They placed the guest book on a different table. Wanda found four ink pens in her car. Ben and Wanda worked well together.

Ben said, "Wanda, you're a very hard worker."

Wanda laughed and said, "I was going to say the same thing about you."

Ben asked, "Do you think it's too cool in here?"

Wanda said, "It is cool. I don't think we should adjust it. It will need to be this cool with the number of people we are expecting."

Ben agreed, "You're right. I think we are finished out here. It looks great. Let's see if they need any help in the kitchen."

Wanda said, "Whatever they are cooking smells wonderful."

Ben laughed and said, "I'm hungry."

Wanda asked, "Do you think we should go get something for everyone to eat for lunch?"

Ben said, "That's a great idea. Let's ask them what they want."

Wanda said, "Sandwiches and chips would be the easiest."

As they walked into the kitchen, everyone was working hard.

Ben said, "Wanda and I were thinking we would go get something for us to eat for lunch."

David said, "That would be great. We're almost finished, I think another hour or so."

Mom asked, "What about some deli sandwiches and potato chips?"

Ben laughed and said, "That's the same thing Wanda suggested. We'll be right back."

Ben said, "I will drive."

Ben opened the passenger door for Wanda.

Wanda said, "Ben, you're such a gentleman."

Ben said, "Yeah, I guess I am."

They talked as they drove to the store. They found all that they needed at the Piggly Wiggly. They even picked up some cookies and some sodas to drink. Everyone took a break to eat lunch. The kitchen was filled with laughter.

Mom said, "I want to thank everyone for the work that you have done today. We have come together as a team. It has been a pleasure working with you all."

Mary said, "I have had a great time and I made some new friends."

Ben said, "Me too."

David said, "I could not have done this by myself. I'm so glad I had you all to help. The food tastes and looks great."

At the end of the day everyone hugged each other and said goodbye.

Ben said, "Wanda, David is going to stop by here in the morning. So, he will need the key to the building. He will drop the key off at Mr. Knowlton's house around ten o'clock."

Wanda said, "That would be great, we will see you all tomorrow."

Wanda, Pam, and Dee waved goodbye and left the building.

Mom said, "Those are some very nice, young ladies."

David said, "Dee is not as bad as I thought. She's still too young for me"

Everyone laughed.

Looking at Ben Mary said, "I saw you and Wanda doing a lot of talking and laughing."

Ben said, "Yes, we did do a lot of talking and laughing."

Mom said, "I'm glad. She's a very nice girl, hard worker, and very pretty."

Ben said, "Yes ma'am she is."

13

THE FUNERAL

Everyone was up early on Saturday morning. Mom prepared a light breakfast, no one was really very hungry.

Mom said, "I know you don't want to eat, but you have to eat something. It will be late before we get a chance to eat again."

David went to go check on the food making sure he had not forgotten anything. He also put the pictures of Grandpa on the table. He then took the key to Wanda at Mr. Knowlton's house.

When it was time to go to the cemetery, Ben drove the car and David drove his truck. David hoped that he would be able to leave early to get to the event center.

The ceremony was scheduled for one o'clock. The family arrived at the grave site at twelve noon. As the car drove through the cemetery, Mary started to cry. Mr. Hick's funeral team was already in place. He showed the family where they would be seated and went over the plan. Reverend King would give a short sermon, but Mr. Hicks did not expect the service to last more than thirty-five minutes. He said usually he would open up the floor for reflections, but with this many people he did not want to take the chance that it would get out of hand.

Mr. Hicks said, "I suggest we have three people do reflections. Ben would you like to say something."

Ben said, "Yes sir, I can."

Mr. Hicks asked, "Who else do you suggest?"

Ben said, "I'm sure Mr. Jennings and Mr. Stevens would like to say something. They have worked the closest with Grandpa."

Mr. Hicks asked, "When you see them, please ask them if they would speak."

Ben said, "Yes, I see both of them now. Excuse me!"

Ben told Mr. Jennings and Mr. Stevens what he needed. They both agreed to speak and thanked Ben for the opportunity. The grave site was starting to fill up. There were so many cars lined up behind each other. Some people had to walk a long distance.

David said, "I may not be able to leave early, I can't get back out because of all of the cars."

Mom pointed west and said, "David, that road over there also leads out of the cemetery. You can go that way."

David relaxed and said, "Thanks, I feel better."

Mom pulled everyone close and said a quick prayer to calm everyone's nerves and emotions. She passed everyone some clean tissue to wipe their eyes if they started to cry.

Mary said, "I may need more than this!"

Everyone laughed.

Grandpa's casket was open for people to view if they wished. There was a line of people walking past the casket. Many nodded their head or smiled at the family. However, some people rolled their eyes when they passed by the family.

Mr. Hicks said, "It is now one o'clock, it's time to start."

Everyone took their seats. All one hundred seats were filled and people were standing all around the grave site.

Ninety percent of the people were white. Of course, that was not a surprise, but some of them were surprised to see four blacks sitting in the family section. Even though Grandpa had been living with the Davis family for a couple of years, not everyone was happy about it.

Reverend King gave a beautiful sermon. Mr. Jennings and Mr. Stevens said wonderful things about Grandpa. Ben talked about how he met Grandpa six years ago and next thing he knew he was part of the family. He talked about how Mr. Cason started out as an employer and mentor, but he ended up being the father figure that he needed.

Many of the people in the audience were in tears. It was a beautiful farewell to a wonderful man. Mr. Hicks invited everyone to the repass that would be held at the new building located at 3232 Highway 15.

David left as soon as he could. The rest of the family stayed to greet some of the congregation. Some people gave them sympathy cards. Some just shook their hands. Surprisingly, there were several people that hugged them and said how happy they were that the Davis' family had been there for Mr. Cason.

After about thirty minutes, Mr. Hicks was finally able to usher the family to their car. When they arrived at the event center, some people were already there. They rushed inside to find at least half of the tables already full.

Mom said, "Plan B! Since, we could not greet them as they came through the door, I want each of us to go to each table and say something nice."

Ben said, "That's a great idea Mom. First, I will go to the kitchen to see how long it will be before the food is ready."

Mom said, "That's fine. Mary, you know how to be nice. Introduce yourself and thank people for coming and let them know that the food will be ready shortly."

Mary said, "No problem, I can do that. I can be gregarious. In which language?"

Ben and Mom laughed.

Mom said, "In English!"

Ben went to the kitchen.

David said, "Everything is running smooth. We will be ready to eat in about seven minutes. All we have to do it put the food on the buffet tables."

Ben looked at Wanda and said, "Wanda, you all look great. The black and white looks very professional."

Wanda smiled.

Ben said, "I have to go greet the people. David, when you are ready, get my attention, I will have Reverend King say grace."

David said, "I have a dinner bell. I will ring it."

Impressed Ben smiled and said, "Wow, great idea."

Ben went in the dining room and found Reverend King. He asked him to stand over near the podium. He told him that when the dinner bell rang, that would be his cue to say grace. Shortly after, David rang the bell.

Reverend King got everyone's attention and prayed over the food. After the prayer, Ben explained which tables would start the buffet line. Ben walked around to see if there were any empty seats. He found one or two empty seats at each table.

Mom said, "I think people have finally stopped coming in."

Mary said, "We forgot to save a place for us to sit and eat."

Mom said, "There are a few empty seats at each table, so just join a table and make conversation. That will give us a chance to get to know these people."

Everything was running smoothly. The servers were moving the people through the line. Everyone was eating.

Ben walked over to Wanda and said, "If you get tired, make sure you take a break."

Wanda said, "I'm fine, but I will watch the others to make sure if I see distress to make them take a break."

Ben said, "OK, some of these people are starting to look alike. I could have sworn that man already went through the line."

Wanda said, "He did. I have seen at least six people come back up already. One man has come up three times."

Ben smiled and said, "I guess they are just hungry. So am I."

Wanda said, "I saved some food for everybody, just in case we did not get a chance to eat."

Ben smiled and said, "Wanda, you're amazing!"

Wanda smiled.

Ben continued to visit each table to make sure everyone was enjoying themselves. Ben, Mom, and Mary never got a chance to sit down to eat, all of the seats were taken.

When most of the people finished eating, Ben went to the podium and said, "Good afternoon everyone. My name is Ben Davis, I am so glad that you were able to come out and celebrate the life of Charlie Cason with us. It has been an emotional week, but we are so thankful that we all were able to come together and celebrate his life. I don't know if all of you know my family. I would like to introduce them. This is my mother, Phyllis Davis. This is my sister, Mary. I would like to introduce to you my brother David. David prepared all of the food that you are enjoying today. Please give him a round of applause for all the work he has done."

Everyone stood up and clapped for David.

Ben continued, "In a few weeks, David will be going back to the Atlanta Institute to continue pursuing his degree in Culinary Arts."

Someone in the audience said, "He can quit now, this food is delicious."

Everyone laughed and agreed. David took a bow.

Ben continued, "I would also like to draw your attention to our wonderful servers. They have done a great job today."

Everyone agreed and clapped.

Ben said, "Finally, I would like to open this time up for a few reflections. If anyone would like to come up and say something about Grandpa, we would love to hear it."

Ten people stood up and walked toward the podium. Each person told a story about their interactions with Mr. Cason. Some were funny. Some of the stories made people sad again.

It was now about 4:30 pm, everyone had eaten. Several people had eaten three times. God multiplied the food, so that everyone was fed.

Ben said, "My family and I would like to thank everyone for coming out today. Your support and attendance are a beautiful display of love for the life of Charlie Cason. We also would like to thank the owner of this establishment. This beautiful event center was exactly what we needed to gather to show our love for Grandpa. Thank you everyone."

People stood up to leave, but no one left. It took another forty-five minutes for the place to empty. Wanda told David to go stand by the door, so people could thank him for the delicious food. Everyone shook his hand and complimented him on his delicious food. One man suggested he bottle that spaghetti sauce and sell it. Many wanted to know if he was available for catering. David explained that he was still in college, but he planned to open a café when he graduated. Finally, everyone was gone.

Mom said, "I have never been part of such an event. I'm so excited. Everything went well."

Mary said, "I enjoyed talking to all of the people."

David said, "I am glad that it is over, but I did enjoy it."

Ben said, "I'm hungry."

Everyone laughed.

David said, "Wanda was wise enough to save food for all of us, let's go fix a plate."

Everyone fixed their plate and came back to the dining room to eat. The sound of chatter, laughter, and exhaustion filled the room.

Mom said, "David, I never doubted that you could cater this event, but now most of the people in Fairville know how capable you are too. Ben, you did a great job as host and representative of the family. I was very proud of you. Mary, many of the people told me how adorable you were. You represented yourself and the family well."

Mom continued, "To the servers, you were amazing. Even Debra and Joyce, you are only twelve and thirteen and you worked just as hard as everyone else. Tammy and Becky, thank you so much for helping out. Wanda, your leadership among the staff was noticeable and truly appreciated. Thank you! I'm so glad that God sent you to Fairville just when we needed you."

Everyone hugged each other.

Ben suggested, "It's late. Let's not try to clean up this afternoon."

David said, "I think we should at least put the plates in the dishwasher."

Mom said, "I think we should also put a load of table cloths in the washing machine. I don't want that spaghetti sauce to stain the new cloths."

Mary said, "There's another washing machine in the next room too, so we can fill up both machines."

Ben said, "OK, if we all work together we can do that in

about thirty minutes. David and I will come back tomorrow to do the rest of the clean-up."

Dee asked, "What time tomorrow? I can come help!"

David smiled and asked, "How about four o'clock?"

Dee smiled and said, "That works for me!"

Everyone snickered as they pulled table cloths from the table. Ben locked up the place and walked the ladies to their car. He opened Wanda's door and said, "Wanda, Mom was right. I'm so glad God sent you here during this time when we needed you."

Wanda said, "I am too!"

Ben said, "Drive carefully. Thanks again."

Ben drove his family home. Everyone was happy to be home. They sat in the living room and talked about the day and how God had come through.

Mary said, "I hope all of my tears are gone."

Mom said, "I'm sure there will be times when you think of Grandpa and get sad. Just remember, that he's in heaven now. Try to focus on the happy times we had with him."

David said, "Right now I am still on a high from all of the nice things people said."

Mom said, "You should be. You're an amazing chef."

Ben said, "Many people asked me if you are still selling cakes."

David asked, "What did you tell them?"

Ben said, "I gave them our phone number and told them to call you."

Everyone laughed.

Mary said, "I would love to be a hostess at a place like the event center."

Mom said, "You just like being the center of attention."

Mary agreed, "Yes, I do!"

Everyone laughed.

Mom asked, "Ben, when will you know who owns the event center?"

Ben said, "I have an appointment with Mr. Jennings on Tuesday. I guess he will tell me then. I need to pay them."

Mom said, "When we pay them, I want to put the payment inside of a nice card thanking them for letting us use the place. When it had not even opened yet."

Ben said, "That's a great idea."

Mary said, "David, I noticed you stopped running away from Dee!"

David laughed and said, "She wore me down! However, she is still too young for me."

Mom said, "She is about four years younger than you. Yes, you are nineteenth and she is fifteen. When you are twenty-five, twenty-one will not seem that young to you."

Everyone laughed.

Mom continued, "Your dad was five years older than me. When we got married, I was nineteen and he was twenty-four."

Mary said, "I did not know that."

Mom said, "He went into the Army right after high school. After serving for four years, he got out. That's when we met. I was in my senior year of high school. He found a job and started to save money. We dated for two years. When he was hired as a truck driver, he asked me to marry him because he could then afford a place for us to live. We were able to get financing for this house. I got a job at the textile factory, next thing you know I was pregnant with Ben. We were married eleven years before he died."

David said, "Wow, I didn't know that either."

Mom said, "So don't count Dee out so fast. However, I don't want you to be surprised if she gets over her crush and falls in love with someone else."

David said, "That's fine with me."

Everyone laughed.

On Sunday after church, Ben opened the golf shop for a few hours. Several customers told him how much they enjoyed the funeral service and repass. Ben thanked everyone for coming. Several customers visited the store. Ben was shocked how busy he was. At four o'clock he closed the shop and drove to the event center. When he arrived, David and Wanda were already there.

Ben apologized, "I'm so sorry for being late. Today was a busy day at the golf shop."

Wanda said, "We understand. We haven't been here long."

Ben unlocked the door and everyone went to work. Dee and David worked together in the kitchen and Ben and Wanda worked together in the dining room. The plan was to clean the place and put things back where they belonged.

Wanda asked, "Did your Grandpa leave you the golf shop?"

Ben said, "Yes."

Wanda said, "That's wonderful. You have your own business already."

Ben said, "I know. I plan to expand the store. There's a vacant building next door. I want to sell other sporting goods."

Wanda said, "That's a great idea. Now, people have to drive to Macon if they want to buy sporting goods."

Ben said, "I know. Of course, this is going to be challenging trying to run the golf shop and open a new store."

Wanda said, "I believe in you."

Surprised Ben asked, "You do?"

Wanda said, "Yes, you're a very hard worker who is intelligent, ambitious, goal oriented, tenacious, and charismatic. I can see that God has blessed you."

Ben said, "I'm still very nervous."

Wanda said, "That's expected. I would be too. Remember, God would not bring you to it, if he was not going to bring you through it."

Ben said, "I agree."

Wanda said, "I thought you said you would be working on your master's degree part time."

Ben said, "I know. I don't know how I'm going to do all of this."

Wanda said, "Well, there's no rush. Take your time. Don't put unnecessary stress on yourself. You may have to hire someone."

Ben said, "That has crossed my mind. I need someone I can trust."

Wanda said, "If you still want to work on your degree, maybe you can take classes one day a week."

Ben said, "I was looking at the Fall Schedule of Classes. I found two graduate courses that both meet on Monday. Each session is three hours. That would make a very long day by the time I drive up in the morning and drive back in the evening."

Wanda said, "Yes, that would be a long day. However, it would only be one day a week."

Ben said, "I know. That's my plan. Only taking two courses a semester, will take me five semesters to finish this degree."

Wanda said encouragingly, "Remember, you're not in a rush."

Ben said, "Thanks for talking this through with me. Are you on track to graduate in May?"

Wanda said excitedly, "Yes I am. I'm getting excited."

Ben said, "That's great. Did you decide to remain a business major?"

Wanda said, "Yes, I did. I'm still not sure where I want to work. If I changed my major, it would delay graduation. I did not want to do that."

Ben laughed and said, "I'm sure it all will work out. You too are a very hard worker, ambitious, intelligent and a very good leader. Your future is bright."

Wanda asked, "Maybe on one of the Mondays that you are on campus we can have lunch."

Ben asked, "Won't your boyfriend get upset?"

Wanda exclaimed, "What boyfriend?"

Ben laughed and said, "Oh, well since you don't have a boyfriend, we can have lunch!"

Wanda laughed and said "Oh, you were trying to be funny. Ha Ha! Miss Tiffany told me that your girlfriend was killed in a car accident. I'm sorry about that."

Ben said, "Yes, that was extremely hard for me. Her name was Tammy. I had planned to ask her to marry me when I graduated."

Wanda said, "I'm sure she was a wonderful woman."

Ben said, "She was. It has been a difficult year. I was just starting to feel normal, then Grandpa died. On Monday, I did not know how I was going to make it."

Wanda said, "I can't imagine."

Ben said, "Truthfully, you being here has helped me a lot. You made a devastating week so much more bearable."

Wanda smiled and said, "I'm so glad. So, are you saying we can possibly have lunch when you are on campus?"

Ben laughed and said, "Yes, I look forward to it."

After everything was cleaned, Ben and Wanda went into the kitchen. It looked shiny and new again. David and Dee were laughing.

David said, "We're finished in here. Everything is back in place, all we have to do is fold up the table cloths."

Ben said, "We're finished too. We can help."

When everything was done, everyone hugged each other

and said goodbye. Ben walked Wanda to her car and opened the door.

Wanda said, "I will be leaving on Saturday to go back home."

Ben said, "I thought you said, you would be here for about a month."

Wanda said, "No, I said, it would take a month for my job to be available. I still need to work, so I need to find another job."

Ben said, "You know right now I need help at the shop. If I offer you a job, can you stay with your uncle for the rest of the summer?"

Wanda asked, "Are you serious?"

Ben exclaimed, "Yes, I'm serious. You have proven that you are a hard worker and you know I need help until I figure everything out."

Wanda laughed and said, "How much does this job pay?"

Ben said, "Minimum wage plus fifty cents."

Wanda said, "That's more than my last job. OK, when do you want me to start?"

Ben said, "Tomorrow at nine o'clock. Now when you come, you need to be ready to work."

Wanda smiled and said, "I will see you then!"

Ben smiled, said goodnight, then closed her car door.

14

THE REVEAL

On Monday, Wanda arrived promptly to work at nine o'clock. Ben smiled and said, "Wow! On time! That's a great habit."

Wanda smiled and said, "I am ready to work."

Ben said, "I need for you to watch the front part of the store and take care of the customers. If you can make sure the bathroom stays clean, dust the displays, and check the customers out. All of the merchandise is kept in the storage room. I will give you a tour of that later."

Wanda said, "No problem."

Ben continued, "We use a regular cash register. I want to upgrade that. So, a copy of the receipt is kept from every transaction and put here."

Wanda asked, "Do you take credit cards?"

Ben said, "Grandpa did not want to start that. I understood, he did not want to learn anything new. That is another upgrade I want."

Wanda asked, "This all seems simple."

Ben said, "Yes, it is. Most of the customers already know

what they want, so we don't do much upselling. We definitely do not tout. There is a 'marked down' table over there. Sometimes, I will make suggestions for them to check it out."

Wanda said, "OK, I can do this."

Ben said, "Of course, I would appreciate any recommendations you may have. If you could start a list, that will help me."

Wanda said, "I have a few in my mind."

Ben said, "I suggested to Grandpa that he close on Monday and Tuesday, because I did not want him working seven days a week. I still plan to close on those days, I just felt that I needed to open this week due to the funeral."

Wanda said, "That's a good plan. You can't work seven days a week."

Ben said, "That will give me Monday to go to class and Tuesday to work on the expansion. I'm supposed to be working on a business plan for the expansion. There are three contractors here in Fairville, I need to call and see if they can give me an estimate for the renovation."

Wanda said, "I can call and schedule them to come out here and look at the space. Do you have the key to the building next door?"

Ben said, "Not yet, I hope to get it tomorrow. I have a meeting with Mr. Jennings, the lawyer. He will explain the legalities of everything."

Wanda said, "I know a girl, she inherited her parent's business when they died. She had to go to probate court to get everything in her name."

Ben said, "I know. I guess that's what he is going to tell me. Since I am changing hours, I also need a simple template that I can put in the window with the store hours. Grandpa was always open, so people did not need to know the hours. When he was not here, they would just come back."

Wanda said, "Dee and I were at the hardware store the other day. We had to pick up some paint for Uncle Robert. I saw a simple template there. You would use a grease pen to write in the hours."

Ben said, "Great, I will go get it. The other thing I wanted to do is prepare a letter and mail it to all of the customers. I started a mailing list about two years ago. In the letter, I wanted to thank everyone for being a loyal customer, thank them for their support of Grandpa, and say something about looking forward to seeing them again soon. At the bottom of the letter, there would be a coupon that they could use on their next visit."

Wanda said, "Now, that's a great idea. That will bring them back to the store."

Ben said, "I know. I need to sit down and write the letter."

Wanda said, "I can draft a letter for you. Do you have a way to get it typed and copied?"

Ben said, "I don't know yet. I will ask Mr. Jennings. I have heard great things about the microcomputer that's becoming popular. One day, I will purchase one."

Wanda asked, "Do you have envelopes to mail the letters."

Ben said, "No, we have never done anything like this before, so there are no office supplies in the shop."

Wanda said, "OK, you are starting from ground zero. That's OK, let's just put these ideas on paper and we can check them off when they are completed."

Ben said, "I know, I don't seem to be organized yet."

Wanda said, "I totally understand. This is the transition from your Grandpa's shop to yours. Some of these things he did not want to do, but you do."

Ben said, "I'm glad you understand, I did not want you to think I was not capable."

Wanda said, "That thought never entered my mind. In a few months, this place will operate as you want it."

Ben said, "Oh, some customers do call. I don't think I will change the name of the shop; so, please answer the phone Cason's Golf Shop."

Wanda asked, "Have you thought of a name for the sporting goods store."

Ben laughed and said, "No, I just decided to do it a week ago, then Grandpa died."

Wanda smiled and said, "We can brainstorm some names later."

Ben said, "I need to go to the hardware store and Dime store to pick up some envelopes. Will you be OK for a little while?"

Wanda smiled and said, "I will be fine."

Ben said, "David made lunch for us, we can eat together later."

Wanda said, "Sounds good."

Ben picked up the template from the hardware store and picked up some office supplies at the Dime Store. When he returned Wanda was checking out a customer, he watched her upsell several items. The customer left with two bags full.

Ben said, "I'm back!"

Wanda said, "Three customers came in while you were gone."

Ben said, "I watched you upsell that man several things. You're amazing."

Wanda said, "I have worked in retail for many years. I think that last man came in wanting just some gloves. He walked out with two pair of gloves, a wristband, and two boxes of golf balls."

Ben laughed and said, "If I had not seen it, I would not believe it."

Wanda said, "This storage room is a work of art."

Ben said, "Thanks, that was one of my first projects. Grandpa gave me free rein to set it up as I saw fit."

Wanda said, "It's impressive. I had no problem finding anything."

Ben added proudly, "It's also set up so I can quickly do inventory."

Wanda said, "That's great. I have had to do inventory in the past and it can be not only difficult but confusing."

Ben said, "I bought some office supplies and the template."

Wanda took the office supplies and found a place for them near the cash register. Ben filled out the template and posted it next to the door. The rest of the day went by fast. Ben and Wanda worked well together.

On Tuesday, Ben felt comfortable leaving Wanda at the store during the time he had his meeting with Mr. Jennings. At 9:55 am, Ben walked into the courthouse. Mr. Jennings's door was closed. His secretary asked him to please have a seat. Shortly after, the door opened and Mr. Jennings ushered a couple out. He smiled at Ben while he finished talking to the couple. Ben waited patiently. As Mr. Jennings walked back toward Ben, his face lit up with a smile.

He said, "Ben, I'm so happy to see you. I truly enjoyed the funeral and the repass. Your family did a great job with everything."

Ben said, "Thank you sir. The building was exactly what we needed."

Mr. Jennings said, "Please come in and have a seat."

Ben said, "Thank you."

Mr. Jennings said, "Ben, I asked you here today for two reasons. One is to make sure you and your family are OK."

Ben said, "We're doing fine. Of course, it has been very

difficult. Planning the funeral and repass last week kept us very busy. This is the first week of us trying to find a new normal."

Mr. Jennings said, "It will take some time. Don't rush it. Grieve when you need to."

Ben said, "My Mom said the same thing."

Mr. Jennings said, "The other reason I needed to see you is to reveal to you exactly what Mr. Cason left you. Do you know what he owned?"

Ben said, "Yes sir, the golf shop, his home, and he told me he purchased the vacant building next door to the golf shop. He wanted me to turn that into a sporting goods shop."

Mr. Jennings asked, "Is there anything else?"

Ben said, "He wrote letters to all of us and in his letter to David, he said that he had purchased the old City Café for him to open his own café. In Mom's letter, he mentioned that he had paid off the mortgage on her house."

Mr. Jennings said, "That is only a small portion of what Mr. Cason owned."

Ben sat up straight and leaned forward.

Mr. Jennings said, "I have a cup of water here and some tissue. You may need it. I don't want you to write down anything that I am telling you today. I will set up a standing meeting on whatever day you want every two weeks. It will take some time for me to explain everything to you. Timothy Stevens will do the same thing. We don't want to overwhelm you, but it will take some time to explain everything to you, so that you will be able to understand."

Ben said, "Truthfully, I am starting to feel overwhelmed now."

Mr. Jennings laughed and said, "I know. I plan to just give you a quick overview today."

Ben said, "OK!"

Mr. Jennings said, "First, I will start with residential

property. You are right, Mr. Cason owned the home he was living in. He also owns about twelve other residential properties in the area."

Ben said, "Twelve!"

Mr. Jennings said, "Yes. Eleven of those properties are currently being rented to tenants. We use a realty company from Macon to manage the properties. Those tenants pay the realty company their rent. The realty company takes care of everything for us. If the property needs to be repaired or updated. The realty company contacts a contractor for us. No one knew that Mr. Cason owned the property, they were leasing."

Ben said, "Are you saying, I now own those properties?"

Mr. Jennings said, "Yes, you do. I suggest we continue to allow the realty company to manage those properties for you. Rent each month is deposited in a specified account and Timothy Stevens keeps track of that."

Ben was silent.

Mr. Jennings said, "So the residential property is pretty simple. You don't have to do anything. That bank account continues to increase because your Grandpa did not touch the money. All of the residential property has been paid for over the years. Timothy pays the taxes and insurance for each property out of that account."

Ben was still in shock.

Mr. Jennings said, "The next section is another simple section. Your Grandpa invested in stocks. He has a diverse portfolio. He has stocks in IBM, Honeywell, Trane Air Conditioning, and many other companies. You don't have to do anything with that either. That takes care of itself. However, anytime that you would like to liquidate some stock or invest in others we can do that."

Ben took a sip of water and said, "Mr. Jennings, this is overwhelming. Are you saying those stocks are mine too!"

Mr. Jennings said, "Yes, they are. Ben, your grandpa was a very rich man. Rough calculations, I would say he was worth about thirty-three million dollars."

Ben stood up and started pacing the floor.

Mr. Jennings said, "Of course, you did not know this. No one in the city knows."

Confused Ben said, "When we were in your office three years ago. Grandpa said, I plan to leave all I have to you, it's not much, but I want you to have it. This is much!"

Mr. Jennings said, "Yes, that is what he said. It took all I had to keep a straight face, you're right 'this is much'."

Ben sat back down, he was speechless.

Mr. Jennings said, "The best way for you to live a normal life is for you to keep what you own a secret too."

Ben said, "No one would believe it anyway."

Mr. Jennings laughed and said, "That is going to be the hard part. As much as you love your family, you can't tell them all of this. Of course, they know about the golf shop, Mr. Cason's house, and the vacant building. But all of the rest, we need to keep it a secret right now. Fairville is not ready for a black, teenage millionaire."

Ben said, "I agree, we can't tell anyone."

Mr. Jennings said, "However, whatever you want to do, you can. We just have to operate in Cognito. Whatever you want to build, we can. We will just do it under a company name, not yours. However, all of the profits belong to you."

Ben asked, "Suppose in the future I get married, would I be able to tell my wife?"

Mr. Jennings said, "Of course you can, but I would not tell her everything at once. Each year just reveal a little at a time."

Ben laughed.

Mr. Jennings said, "The next section is commercial or industrial property. Your grandpa owned nine commercial buildings in town and one industrial site. You know about the golf shop, the vacant building, and the city café. What you don't know about is the Dime Store, Maxwell's Store, Rexall Drug Store, the laundry mat, the old movie theater and the dry cleaners. He did not buy them all at one time. Whenever a company was going out of business, he would help them out by purchasing the property. Now he does not own the companies. The company pays monthly fees to rent the space. The industrial site is the textile mill on the north side of town. The current company took over the operation of factory, but they do not own the site. They pay a substantial fee each month to use the site. There is also about one hundred acres of vacant land throughout the county. There is one more commercial property. It is very new. Mr. Cason came to me with the idea when Tammy visited about two years ago."

Ben was quiet.

Mr. Jennings said, "Tammy wanted to run an event center, Mr. Cason felt that you were going to ask Tammy to marry you. So, he started building the event center on Highway 15, he wanted to give it to you as a wedding gift."

Ben started to cry. He could not hold back his tears.

Mr. Jennings said, "So the building you used to have the repass for your grandfather, you own."

Ben cried even louder. Mr. Jennings stood up and walked closer to Ben to hug him. Ben stood up and hugged Mr. Jennings.

Mr. Jennings said, "Your grandfather loved you very much Ben. He could have donated a lot of his estate to charity, but he wanted you to have it. He told me that you would take it to the next level. That whatever he was worth, that he knew you would double if not triple it."

Ben pulled himself together and said, "Mr. Jennings, this is truly overwhelming."

Mr. Jennings said, "I know. I also know that the hard part is keeping it a secret. Your grandfather felt that Fairville should know about the event center. I agree. So, the properties you need to actively manage are the golf shop, the sporting goods store, and the event center. Oh, the house, whatever you want to do with that is up to you."

Ben said, "Before the house can be rented, it has to be emptied. I am not ready to deal with the house yet. Do we have to do anything with it right now?"

Mr. Jennings said, "No, we do not. We will continue to pay the utilities, insurance, and everything else out of the rental property account until you are ready. Remember you don't have to empty it, we can hire someone to do it for you."

Ben said, "No sir. I want to go through Grandpa's things myself."

Mr. Jennings said, "That will be fine."

Ben begged, "Please tell me that's all. I don't think I can take anymore."

Mr. Jennings smiled and said, "There are a few more things. There are several bank accounts. Timothy Stevens will fill you in on the balances of those accounts and what they are used for. Mr. Cason's personal account now belongs to you, I think it has at least $200,000 in it."

Ben exclaimed, "Two hundred thousand dollars in his personal account! Oh, my goodness!"

Mr. Jennings said, "I told you that your grandfather was a very rich man."

After drinking some more water, Ben asked, "Do we have

to go to probate court for all of this to be transferred in my name?"

Mr. Jennings said, "That is a very intelligent question. The answer is no. Mr. Cason did not want you to have to worry about probate court. He went through that with his father. Remember all of that paperwork I had you sign."

Ben said, "Yes sir."

Mr. Jennings said, "That paperwork set you up as a partner on all of your grandfather's accounts, businesses, properties, etc. So, when I get a copy of the death certificate, his name will be taken off and only your name will remain."

Ben started crying again.

Mr. Jennings said, "I know this is a lot, but Ben you can handle it. God has blessed you abundantly. He would not bring you to it, if he did not plan to bring you through it."

Ben said, "I'm speechless. Grandpa was always thinking of me and my family."

Mr. Jennings said, "He loved you all very much. I knew him before you started working for him and he was not a happy man. He was very sad and lonely after his wife died. After you started working for him, I could see a renewed spirit. He was not only happy, but he started living with a purpose again."

Ben said, "I tried so hard to show him that I loved him."

Mr. Jennings said, "You succeeded. That's why all of this has been saved for you."

Ben said, "Grandpa told me that if ever I needed anything or had any questions, that I should come to you."

Mr. Jennings said, "That is true. Do you have any questions?"

Ben said, "I need some time to digest all that you have told me. I had a few questions before I came in concerning the vacant building."

Mr. Jennings said, "Oh, thank you for bringing that up. Here are your keys."

Ben took the keys and said, "Thank you. Do you have a contractor that you can recommend to give me an estimate of what it would cost to renovate?"

Mr. Jennings said, "Your grandfather worked with two. I have their cards right here. One is Daniel Trotter and the other is Frank McCants. He always got estimates from both for whatever he wanted to do."

Ben took the cards and said, "Thank you. I also need to write a business plan for the renovation."

Mr. Jennings said, "I have this business plan guide. I use it all the time. You can borrow it."

Ben took the guide and said, "This really helps. The last thing is that I wanted to send out letters to the golf shop customers thanking them for supporting Grandpa over the years. Who would I get to type the letter and print copies for me. I bought some envelopes to mail them in."

Mr. Jennings smiled and said, "You are welcome to use my secretary for any administrative work you may need. Just bring her the draft of the letter and the addresses. She will type the letters and mail them out for you."

Ben said, "Oh, that's a big help. I received a scholarship to get my master's degree. I plan to work on it only part time. This fall I will be taking two classes on Monday. I thought it was a good idea before you told me about all of this."

Mr. Jennings said, "I think it's a great idea. Part time? It will take you about five semesters, before you know, it will be over. You can also get a better understanding of all that me and Timothy will be telling you. I believe in education. That will only help you take your grandfather's investments to the next level."

Ben said, "Yes, sir."

Mr. Jennings said, "I have one more thing for you. Your grandfather gave me this letter to give you after I told you everything."

Ben took the sealed letter and said, "During his last days, I saw him writing a lot. I wondered what he was writing but I did not ask."

Mr. Jennings said, "Yes, he had time to think about all that he wanted for you and your family since you had loved him back to life."

Ben stood up and said, "Thank you so much for everything."

Mr. Jennings said, "How about we meet every other Thursday. Would you like to have the meetings early or late?"

Ben said, "If we could meet before I opened the shop, that would be great."

Mr. Jennings asked, "Would eight o'clock be too early for you?"

Ben said, "No sir. That is perfect. Oh, I have hired some summer help. How do I pay her? Grandpa gave me cash every Friday for the hours I worked."

Mr. Jennings said, "Timothy will be able to help you with that. I'm sure he will recommend payment from the golf shop account. He will cut the checks for you. I think your grandfather just paid you out of his personal account. Oh, and I wanted to congratulate you."

Confused Ben said, "Congratulate me!"

Mr. Jennings said, "Yes, Timothy told me that for the last six years that you have worked at the golf shop, the profit margins have skyrocketed. Continue to do what you are doing, you are doing a great job."

Ben said, "Thank you sir. I have a few more ideas."

Mr. Jennings said, "I am sure you do. Have a great day."

15

SHARING THE NEWS

The sun was shining bright on that July summer day when Ben left the courthouse. He sat on a park bench outside of the courthouse reflecting on what just happened to him. He thanked God for the abundant blessings that he had bestowed upon him. He asked God to give him wisdom to manage these blessings. He asked for strength because he still felt overwhelmed. He then asked God to allow him to continue to be a blessing to others. After his prayer he felt a sense of peace.

He remembered that three people had said the same thing to him. First, it was his mother. She said, 'if God brings you to it, he will bring you through it.' Wanda said the same thing to him the other day, then Mr. Jennings repeated the same phrase a few moments ago. He was now starting to believe it. God had sent him the same message three times. That was truly confirmation.

He reflected on all that had happened in the last week. He was glad he could not tell it all, because no one would believe it. He realized that keeping it a secret was protection. He had read about people being targeted because of their success.

As he looked at the last letter from Grandpa, he said aloud, "Grandpa, I can't read this letter right now. I need some time to just process everything. I thank you for everything, and I will work hard to continue to make you proud."

Ben stood up, put the letter in his pocket, wiped his tears and headed to the golf shop. When he arrived, there were several customers in the shop.

Ben walked in the front door and said, "Good morning everyone."

One customer replied, "Good morning Ben, will you be keeping the golf shop open since your grandfather died?"

Ben said, "Yes sir. We will stay open. Did you find everything you needed?"

The customer smiled and said, "Yes I did. Wanda even suggested some things that I did not know I needed."

Ben said, "Great, it's great seeing you again."

Another customer walked up to Ben and said, "I'm glad you are keeping the shop open. I know a few people, they don't plan to shop here anymore. I like shopping here."

Ben smiled and said, "I am glad."

Finally, all of the customers left the shop, Ben said, "Wanda, you are a natural at this."

Wanda said, "All of my summer jobs have been at some type of retail facility. So, I have a lot of experience."

Ben said, "You remember, you asked me if we could have lunch whenever I was on campus."

Wanda said, "Yes!"

Ben said, "I don't want to wait. Would you go on a real date with me before then?"

Wanda smiled and said, "I would love too!"

Ben asked, "Is there anything particular you would like to do?"

Wanda said, "No, not really, I'm a very simple girl. I just like spending time with you. So, whatever you chose would be fine."

Ben smiled and said, "OK, I was thinking either this Friday or Saturday. Which day do you like best?"

Wanda said, "Truthfully, I would like both!"

With a bigger smile on his face, Ben said, "I would like that too. I will plan something."

Wanda said, "Great!"

Pulling the keys out of his pocket he said, "My meeting with Mr. Jennings went great. I have the keys to the building next door. I also have business cards for the two contractors that Grandpa used."

Wanda asked, "Is one of those contractors Daniel Trotter?"

Ben replied, "Yes, how did you know?"

Wanda said, "I called him; he will come by tomorrow to look at the building."

Ben said, "I should not be surprised. Did you contact anyone else?"

Wanda said, "No, I haven't had time. I got busy with customers."

Looking at the business card Ben said, "Well, the other contractor is Frank McCants."

Wanda took the business card and said, "I will call and set something up for him too."

Ben said, "Thanks! I also got a Business Plan guide to help me write the business plan. Mr. Jennings let me borrow it."

Wanda took the book, turning it over she said, "I will try to find this book and order it. You may need it again in the future, then you won't have to borrow it."

Ben said, "Great idea. I have some really good news I want to tell you now."

Wanda smiled and said, "Wow, I can see that you're excited." Ben said, "You know the nice place, where we had Grandpa's repass."

Wanda laughed and said, "Of course, the building with no name!"

Ben said, "Grandpa built that building. It now belongs to me!" Wanda said excitedly, "Ben, that's wonderful. I can't believe it."

Ben said, "It took me a while to believe it too."

Wanda asked, "Why did he build the building?"

Ben said, "Grandpa knew that I planned to ask Tammy to marry me when I graduated from college. I never told him, but he knew. Tammy wanted to be an event planner. As a wedding gift to us, he started construction on the building. Of course, then Tammy died. He completed the building earlier this year. So now, it's mine."

Wanda asked, "He did not tell you anything about the building?"

Ben said, "No. I guess he was waiting for me to get over Tammy."

Wanda asked, "Are you over her?"

Ben said, "Yes, I am. Grandpa kept telling me to keep my heart open, that God had someone else for me."

Wanda said, "I'm so happy for you Ben. This is big. Now, you will have three businesses! The golf shop, the sporting goods store, and the event center."

Ben said, "I know. I was frazzled yesterday. This morning I was truly overwhelmed, so I prayed. Now, I have a sense of peace. Yes, I have a lot of work to do, but I can do it!"

Wanda hugged Ben and said, "I know you can!"

Ben asked, "What do you think we should call the event center?"

Wanda said, "Wow! I don't know. Let me get a pad of paper and we can brainstorm some ideas."

Ben said, "The event center in Macon where Tammy worked was called Walton's Event Center. Eve Walton owned the place."

Wanda said, "That's kind of boring. We have an event center in Warner Robins it was called Celebrations."

Ben said, "That's different. Let's include Grandpa's name on it."

Wanda asked, "You don't want to use Tammy's name?"

Ben said, "No, I don't think so. I'm moving forward. I want to use Grandpa's name."

Wanda asked, "What about Cason Event Center?"

Ben said, "Like you said, boring. This center will help people celebrate things."

Wanda asked, "What about Cason's Celebration Center?"

Ben said, "That's it. I love it. Cason's Celebration Center. It has a nice ring to it and it will help people remember Grandpa!"

Wanda said, "I like it too!"

Ben said, "Thank you so much for your help in everything Wanda."

Wanda said, "It's truly a pleasure. I'm enjoying it all."

Ben said, "David made us lunch again. Are you hungry?"

Wanda said, "Surprisingly, I am not. I guess I'm just excited. However, we better eat now, customers will be coming in soon."

Ben and Wanda worked the rest of the day. After work, Ben headed home to tell his family the good news about the event center. When he arrived home, Mary and David ran out to meet him.

David said, "The phone has been ringing all day. I have so many cake orders."

Mary said, "I won't be able to help him, remember I leave this Saturday to go to camp in Athens!"

Ben said, "David, that's wonderful. I am not surprised. I gave the phone number out to at least ten people."

David exclaimed, "And all of them have called."

Ben said, "Mary, I had forgotten about your camp. How long will you be gone?"

Mary said, "Two weeks, I know that I will miss you all, but I'm excited."

David said, "I plan to drive her up, I know you have to work."

As they were walking into the house Ben said, "Thanks."

Shortly after Mom drove up, everyone went outside to meet her.

Smiling as she got out of the car, Mom said, "There are my beautiful children."

Everyone greeted Mom and gave her a hug.

David said, "Dinner will be ready in about ten minutes."

Mom said, "That's fine. You know, I really like driving myself to work. I stop by the rideshare and pick up people on my way to work and I drop them off after work. Many people try to give me gas money. I tell them no thank you. I was already going this way. I'm just so happy to be able to give back. God sent people to give me a ride when I needed it; I want to do the same."

Everyone smiled.

When everyone was seated at the table, Mom said, "I know that Grandpa's empty seat is a constant reminder. Do you all want to move it?"

Mary said, "I don't!"

David said, "Neither do I. I like looking at it. It makes me happy when I think of him. I'm not sad anymore."

Ben said, "I agree. I want to leave it there too!"

Mom said, "I feel the same way. I just wanted to make sure you all were comfortable."

Ben asked, "David, what are we eating?"

David laughed and said, "I'm experimenting with casseroles. This is a cheesy, chicken casserole. It has chicken, vegetables, cheese, and pasta. I'm also practicing making biscuits. What do you think?"

After tasting the casserole Ben said, "I like it. There are a lot of vegetables in here. I see mushrooms, tomatoes, and something else."

Mom asked, "Is that zucchini?"

David said, "Yes, it is."

Mary said, "I like it too. Your biscuits are very good, please pass me the jelly!"

Mom said, "Your biscuits are very light, not heavy. What did you do differently?"

David proudly said, "I used cold butter!"

Ben said, "You don't need to practice any more, this is delicious."

With her mouth full Mom said, "I agree. OK, let's go around the table. Mary, you start. What's going on?"

Wiping her mouth, Mary said, "Today was my last day at work, the high school library is updated with new books. I'm excited about leaving for camp on Saturday."

Mom said, "I'm excited for you too. I will miss you though."

Mary said, "I know! I will call and write."

Ben said, "You are going to have a great time."

Mary said, "I wish that Becky was going, but I'm OK going by myself. I look forward to meeting new friends."

Everyone laughed.

Mom asked, "David, when will you head back to Atlanta?"

David said, "In about two more weeks, I will be able to

pick Mary up from camp on that Friday. On that Sunday, I will head back. I can't believe this will be my second year. Time is going by so fast."

Mom said, "I know. I have been working at the textile factory for twenty years. Sometimes, it seems like a long time, but other days it seems like it was just yesterday."

Ben asked, "Mom, are you eligible for retirement?"

Mom said, "Yes, I guess I am, but I plan to keep working. How is work going at the shop?"

Ben said, "Wanda is an amazing worker. She has vast retail experience, so she's helping me a lot."

Mary laughed and said, "Amazing! That's a strong word. I can tell that you like Wanda!"

Everyone laughed.

Ben said, "Yes, I do Mary. I did not think I would like anyone else again after Tammy, but I do like Wanda very much. I asked her to go on a date with me this weekend?"

Mary exclaimed, "I knew it. What day Friday or Saturday?"

Ben smiled and said, "Both!"

Everyone laughed.

Mom said, "We all like Wanda too. She is not only wise, but unselfish. She tries to help whenever she can, that's a great trait."

Ben said, "Yes, she does. I went to talk to Mr. Jennings today."

Mom asked, "Did you find out who owns the event center?"

Ben said, "Yes, I did. You remember when Tammy came to visit and she said that she wanted to work at an event center."

Everyone put down their forks to listen.

Ben continued, "Well, Grandpa knew that I was going to ask Tammy to marry me after I graduated from college. So as a wedding gift, he started building the event center. But when

Tammy died, he did not mention it. He just saved it. So, the event center belongs to me!"

Mom stood up and said, "What! That's wonderful!"

Mary jumped up and said, "I can't believe it. I can't believe it!"

David asked, "Ben, are you serious? You're not joking, are you?"

Ben said, "Yes, I am serious."

Mom said, "This is great news. I don't know what to say!"

Ben said, "It has taken me a while to adjust to the idea too."

Mom said, "Grandpa was so generous. That is a gift that keeps on giving."

David said, "When I open my café, I can start a catering business too for the event center."

Mom said, "This is big, really big. OK, let's calm down. Everyone let's hold hands, we have to pray. God, thank you so much for all that you are doing for our family. We thank you for bringing Dad into our lives, we love him. We also thank you for using him to set up a beautiful future for us. Help us to be good stewards over everything you are providing for us. In Jesus name we pray. Amen!"

Everyone said, "Amen!"

Mom said, "It's going to take some time to adjust to this idea."

Mary asked, "What will you call the center? We have to put a sign out front."

Ben said, "Wanda helped me brainstorm some names. What do you think about Cason's Celebration Center?"

Mom said, "I love it!"

Mary said, "I love it too!"

David said, "It's a great name. It gives honor to Grandpa and lets people know that this place will be used to celebrate things. I like it."

Mom said, "I can't believe it. This is overwhelming."

Ben said, "Mom, this morning I truly felt overwhelmed. I am adjusting. You told me that if God brings you to it, he will bring you through it."

Mom said, "I believe that!"

Ben said, "I do too. So, I'm not feeling as overwhelmed as I was feeling earlier."

Mary said, "Ben, it's going to be hard for you to run the golf shop, the sporting goods store, and the celebration center."

Ben said, "I know. Mom, would you consider retiring and managing the celebration center for me?"

David exclaimed, "That's a wonderful idea!"

Mom said, "Wow, I don't know anything about running an event center!"

Ben said, "We will learn together!"

Mary said, "Mom, say yes. You know I want to be a hostess there."

Everyone laughed.

Mom said loudly, "Yes! I would love to run the celebration center."

Everyone jumped up and said, "Yay! Yay!"

After dinner, Ben was sitting on the porch thinking about all that had happened today.

He said, "God, I can't thank you enough for the blessings you have bestowed upon me and my family. Please, continue to order my steps."

Ben reached into his pocket to retrieve the last letter from Grandpa.

He said, "Grandpa, I am still not ready to read this. I'm still trying to adjust to all that has been saved for me. I promise to read it soon!"

To be continued…

Continue on this amazing journey with Ben as he discovers all that God has saved for him. Order today:

Book 1 Saved for Ben   ISBN 978-1-6642-6888-3

Book 2 Saved for Ben: The College Years   ISBN 978-1-6642-6892-0

Book 3 Saved for Ben: Ben and Wanda   ISBN 978-1-6642-6895-1

Book 4 Saved for Ben: The Legacy   ISBN 978-1-6642-6898-2

Stay tuned for the continuing saga!

Printed in the United States
by Baker & Taylor Publisher Services